The Last Day of
a Condemned Man

The Last Day of
a Condemned Man

Victor Hugo

Translated by Christopher Moncrieff

ALMA CLASSICS

ALMA CLASSICS
an imprint of

ALMA BOOKS LTD
Thornton House
Thornton Road
Wimbledon Village
London SW19 4NG
United Kingdom
www.101pages.co.uk

The Last Day of a Condemned Man first published in 1829
This translation first published by Alma Classics in 2009
Reprinted October 2009, 2011
A new edition first published by Alma Classics in 2013. Repr. 2018
This new edition first published by Alma Classics in 2021
English Translation and Notes © Christopher Moncrieff, 2009

Cover: nathanburtondesign.com

Printed in Great Britain by CPI Group (UK) Ltd, Croydon CR0 4YY

ISBN: 978-1-84749-870-0

Contents

The Last Day of a Condemned Man

Preface to the 1832 Edition   III

A Comedy About a Tragedy   XXIII

The Last Day of a Condemned Man   1

Claude Gueux   67

Note on the Text   93

Notes   95

Preface to the 1832 Edition

E ARLY EDITIONS OF THIS WORK, initially published without the author's name, began with just the following few lines:

> *There are two ways of taking account of this book's existence. Either to see it as a bundle of rough, yellowed sheets of paper on which the last thoughts of a poor wretch were found written down one by one; or as the work of a man, a dreamer who spends his time observing nature in the name of art, a philosopher, a poet – who knows – from whose imagination this idea came and who seized upon it, or rather let himself be seized by it, and could only shake it off by putting it into a book.*
>
> *Of these two explanations the reader will choose whichever one he wishes.*

As can be seen, at the time of the book's first publication the author did not feel it was the right moment to say everything that was on his mind. He preferred to wait until it was understood, to see if it would be. It was. The author can now reveal the political idea, the social idea that he wanted to make public in this frank and innocent literary guise. So he states, or rather openly admits, that *The Last Day of a Condemned Man* is nothing other than an appeal – direct or indirect, however you wish to see it – for the abolition of the death penalty. What his intention was, what he would like future generations to see in this work, if they ever interest themselves with so minor a thing, is not the specific defence of some particular criminal, some defendant of his own choosing, which is always both simple and short-lived: it is an overall and ongoing plea for every defendant now and in the future; it is the great point of law of humanity put forward in a loud, clear voice to that great Court of Appeal called society; it is the hour of reckoning for point-blank refusals, *abhorrescere a sanguine,** set up for all time before every criminal trial; it is the sombre and fatal question that pulses obscurely deep down inside every vital cause, beneath that triple layer of pathos that shrouds magistrates' blood-soaked rhetoric; it is a question of life and death I tell you, naked, laid bare, stripped of the high-sounding artifices of the public prosecutor, dragged brutally up to date and put where it can be seen, where it should be, where it actually is, in its proper place, its hideous place, not in the courtroom but on the scaffold, not before the judge but before the executioner.

This is what he wanted to do. If in the future he were to be praised for having done so, something he dared not hope for, then he could not wish for any other laurels.

So he states it, repeats it, makes it his business in the name of every defendant, before every court, every bench, every jury, every form of justice. This book is addressed to each and every judge. And for the appeal to be as far-reaching as the cause – and this is why *The Last Day of a Condemned Man* is the way it is – he had to prune his subject matter of anything unpredictable, of the accidental, the particular, the special, the relative, the changeable, the episode, the anecdote, the special event, the proper name, and confine himself (if that is what it is to confine yourself) to pleading the cause of any condemned man executed on any day for any crime. Happy if, with no assistance other than that of his thoughts, he has delved deep enough to draw blood from the heart of the magistrate beneath his *æs triplex!** Happy if he has shown that those who think themselves just are pitiful! Happy if by scratching the surface of a judge he has occasionally managed to find a man!

When this book was published three years ago a few people thought it worthwhile to question whether it was the author's idea. Some of them assumed it was an English book, others that it was American. It seems strange to go a thousand miles to look for the origins of something, to find the source of the stream that runs past your door in the River Nile. Sadly this is neither an English book, nor American, nor Chinese. The author didn't get the idea for *The Last Day of a Condemned Man* from a book, he is not in the habit of travelling all that distance to get ideas, but somewhere where all of you can get them – perhaps where you did get them (for who has not lived or dreamt *The Last Day of a Condemned Man?*) – quite simply, on the Place de Grève.* That is where, walking past one day, he found this fatal idea lying in a pool of blood beneath the reddened stumps of the guillotine.

Ever since then, every time the day came when, according to the whim of those mournful Thursdays in the Court of Appeal, the cry of a death sentence being announced was heard in Paris; every time the author heard those hoarse yells that draw onlookers to La Grève go by under his window; every time that painful idea came back to him, seized hold of him, filled his head with policemen, headsmen and crowds, described the final sufferings of the wretched dying man to him hour by hour – at this moment he is making his last confession, at this moment they are cutting his hair, at this moment they are binding his hands – summoned him, the poor poet, to tell all this to a society that was going about its business while this monstrous thing was being carried out, urged him, drove him on, shook him, dragged the lines from his mind when he was in the midst of writing them and killed them off barely drafted, blocked out all his work, got in the way of everything, besieged him, haunted him, assailed him. It was torture, a torture that began at daybreak and lasted, like that of the poor wretch who was being tortured at the same moment, until *four o'clock*. Only then, once the grim voice of the clock called out the *ponens caput expiravit*,* did the author breathe, regain some independence of thought. Finally one day, as far as he can remember it was the one after Ulbach's execution,* he began to write this book. After that he felt better. Whenever one of those State crimes that go by the name of legal executions was committed, his conscience told him he was no longer part of it, and he no longer felt on his forehead that drop of blood which spurts from La Grève onto the head of every member of society.

But it was not enough. Washing your hands is good, preventing blood from flowing would be better.

Then would he not have the highest, holiest, most noble aim: to contribute to the abolition of the death penalty? For does he not wholeheartedly endorse the wishes and efforts of those high-minded men from every country who have been trying to topple that sinister tree for years, the only tree that revolutions do not uproot? So he is delighted to take his turn, he who is so puny, to strike his blow, to do his best to deepen the incision that, sixty-six years ago, Beccaria* made into the old gibbet that has loomed over Christianity for centuries.

We have just said the scaffold is the only edifice that revolutions do not tear down. It is true that revolutions are rarely abstemious when it comes to human blood, and given that they exist to prune, lop, to deadhead society, the death penalty is one implement that they find it most difficult to part with.

Yet we admit that if ever a revolution appeared capable and worthy of abolishing the death penalty, it was the July Revolution. It really seemed to fall to the most humane popular movement of modern times to do away with the barbaric punishment of Louis XI, Richelieu and Robespierre, to stamp the inviolability of human life into the law's brow. 1830 deserved to break the blade of '93.

For a moment we hoped. In August 1830 there was so much kindness and compassion in the air, the masses had such a spirit of gentleness and civilization, you could feel your heart swell at the sight of such a fine future, that we thought the death penalty had been abolished then and there by natural right, by unanimous and tacit consent like all the other bad things that had been upsetting us. The people had just made a bonfire with the rags of the Ancien Régime. This one was the blood-soaked rag. We thought it was in the pile. We thought it had been burnt with the rest. And for a few weeks, confident and trusting, we had faith in a future where life was as inviolable as liberty.

And it is true that barely two months went by before an attempt was made to turn Cesare Bonesana's magnificent legal utopia into a reality.

Sadly it was a clumsy attempt, ill-considered, almost hypocritical, and done for motives other than that of the general good.

In October 1830, if we remember rightly, a few days after issuing an order of the day to set aside the proposal to bury Napoleon under the column,* the entire Chamber began to weep and wail. The question of the death penalty was raised – we'll say a few words about the actual circumstances in a moment – and it was as if the legislators' very souls had suddenly been seized by a wonderful spirit of forgiveness. Everyone competed to speak, to groan, to raise their hands to heaven. The death penalty? Good God! How appalling! An elderly public prosecutor, white in his red robes, who had eaten bread dipped in the blood of arraignments all his life, suddenly put on a shamefaced expression and called the gods to witness that he found the guillotine an affront. For two days the gallery was full of tearful mob orators. It was a lament, a myriology,* a concert of mournful psalms, a *Super flumina Babylonis*, a *Stabat Mater dolorosa*, a great symphony in C with choirs played by this orchestra of speakers who fill the front benches of the Chamber and produce such fine sounds on big days. One had a bass voice, another a falsetto. Nothing was lacking. You could not have asked for anything with more pathos and poignance. The evening session was particularly emotional, well-meaning and heart-rending like a last act by La Chaussée. The members of the public, who couldn't understand a word, had tears in their eyes.*

So what was it about? Abolishing the death penalty?

Yes and no.

Here are the facts:

Four gentlemen,* four upstanding men, the sort of men you might meet in a drawing room and with whom you may have exchanged a few polite words; four of these men, I tell you, had tried to stage one of those daring coups in the upper reaches of government which Bacon calls a *crime* and Machiavelli a *venture*. But whether crime or venture, the law, which is savage with everyone, punishes it with death. And there they were, the four of them, prisoners, captives of the law, guarded by three hundred tricolour cockades beneath the lovely arches of Vincennes. What to do and how? You realize it is impossible to send them to La Grève in a tumbril, bound disgracefully with rough cord, back to back with that public servant who simply must not be named, not four men like you and me, four *gentlemen?* Even more so if there is a mahogany guillotine waiting there!

Well then! All we have to do is abolish the death penalty!

And with that the Chamber got to work.

But note, Messieurs, that only yesterday you were calling this abolition utopia, a theory, a dream, madness, a piece of poetry. Note that this is not the first time we have tried to draw your attention to the tumbril, to the rough cords and the terrible scarlet machine, and so it is odd that this hideous contraption should suddenly be so obvious to you.

So that is what this is really about! It is not for you, the people, that we are abolishing the death sentence, but for us, deputies who might become ministers. We can't have Guillotin's machine biting the upper classes. We will smash it. All the better if it suits everybody, but we were only thinking of ourselves. Ucalegon is burning.* Put out the fire. Quick, get rid of the executioner, change the penal code.

And that is how a self-seeking hotchpotch distorts and debases the very finest social schemes. It is the black vein in white marble; it gets everywhere, appears under your chisel at any moment without warning. Your statue has to be redone.

There is naturally no need to say that we were not among those who demanded the four ministers' heads. Once these hapless individuals were arrested, our angry indignation at their attempted coup changed to heartfelt pity, as it did for everyone else. We remembered the prejudices that some of them had been brought up with, the limited mind of their leader, a stubborn and relapsed fanatic left over from the conspiracies of 1804, hair turned prematurely white from the damp darkness of prison, the deadly necessities of their position, the impossibility of halting the rapid downwards slide on which the monarchy had launched itself flat out on 8th August 1829, the influence of royalty which up till then we had taken too little account of, especially the dignity that one of them spread over their misfortune like a purple cloak. We were among those who genuinely wanted them to be spared, and were prepared to devote ourselves to that. If by some remote chance a scaffold had ever had to be set up for them on La Grève, we are in no doubt – and if we are deluding ourselves we don't wish to stop – we are in no doubt there would have been a riot to tear it down, and the writer of these lines would have been among that holy riot. Because, and this has to be said as well, during any social crisis, of all scaffolds the political scaffold is the most monstrous, the most harmful, the most pernicious, the one that most needs eradicating. That type of guillotine takes root under the pavements and soon shoots up everywhere.

During any revolution beware the first head that rolls. It gives the people an appetite.

So personally we agreed with those who wanted to spare the four ministers, agreed in every way for emotional as well as political reasons. But we would have preferred the Chamber to find a different occasion to suggest abolishing the death penalty.

If they had suggested this desirable abolition, not in the case of four ministers who fell from the Tuileries into Vincennes, but that of the first highwayman to come along, or one of those wretches whom you barely notice when they pass you in the street, whom you don't speak to, whose dusty clothes you instinctively avoid brushing against; unfortunates who spent their ragged childhood barefoot in muddy streets, shivering on the embankments in winter, warming themselves outside the kitchen windows at Monsieur Véfour's where you have dinner, rooting out a crust here and there from piles of refuse and cleaning it up before eating it, scratching about in the gutter all day with a nail to find a farthing, having no other amusement except the free entertainment on the King's birthday and executions on the Place de Grève, that other free show; poor devils whom hunger drives to stealing, and stealing to everything else; the deprived children of a cruel mother society whom the workhouse takes at twelve, the penal colony at eighteen, the scaffold at forty; wretches whom with schooling and a trade you could have turned to the good, made virtuous, useful, but whom you don't know what to do with, shedding them like a useless burden, either to the ants' nest at Toulon or the silent enclosure at Clamart,* cutting off their lives after taking away their freedom. If it had been for one of these people you suggested abolishing the death penalty, then oh how truly honourable, great, holy, magnificent, revered your session would have been! Ever since the venerable Fathers at Trent invited heretics to the Council in the name of God's vital organs, *per viscera Dei*, in the hope they would be converted, *quoniam sancta synodus sperat hæreticum conversionem,** never has a gathering of men offered a more sublime, splendid, more merciful sight to the world. It has always been for those who are truly strong, truly great, to show concern for the poor and weak. It would be a fine thing for a committee of Brahmins to take up the outcast's cause. And in this case the outcast's cause was the people's cause. By abolishing the death penalty for its own sake, without waiting till you were personally involved with the matter, you would be performing more than a political task: you would be performing a social task.

Yet you did not even perform a political task by trying to abolish it: it was not to abolish it but just to save four unfortunate ministers who had been caught red-handed in a coup d'état!

And what happened? Well, since you were not genuine we became suspicious. When people realized you were trying to put them off the scent they lost their temper with the whole idea and, extraordinary thing, fought for the death penalty although they are the ones who bear the brunt of it. That is what your blunder led to. By approaching the matter from the wrong angle, and insincerely, you jeopardized it for a long time to come. You put on an act. You got booed.

Despite this hoax a few people were good enough to take it seriously. Straight after the famous session, an order was given to public prosecutors by a minister of justice, a decent man, to suspend all executions indefinitely. On the face of it it was a great step forwards. The opponents of the death penalty could breathe again. But their illusions were short-lived.

The ministers' trial came to its conclusion. I don't know what the verdict was. Their lives were spared. Ham* was chosen as a compromise between death and liberty. Once the various arrangements had been made the men in government forgot any fear they had had, and with fear went humanity. There was no longer any question of abolishing capital punishment; and once there was no need of it, utopia became utopia again, theory theory, poetry poetry.

Yet there were still a few unfortunate common convicts who had been pacing round exercise yards for five or six months, breathing the fresh air, minds at rest, confident of living and taking their reprieve as a pardon. But wait.

To be honest the executioner had been very afraid. The day he heard the lawmakers talking humanity, philanthropy, progress, he had thought he was lost. The wretch hid himself away, huddled up under his guillotine, as uneasy in the July sunshine as a nightbird in the daytime, trying hard to be forgotten, putting his hands over his ears and not daring to breathe. He was not seen for six months. He gave no sign of life. Yet in his dark place he gradually felt reassured. He had been listening outside the Chamber and had not heard his name mentioned again. No more of those grand high-sounding words that gave him such a fright. No more bombastic statements from *On Crimes and Punishments.** They were attending to quite different things now: a serious social interest, some byroad, a subsidy for the Opéra-Comique or a heavy loss of a hundred thousand francs out of a frenzied budget of fifteen hundred million. No one was thinking about him now, the head-chopper. Seeing this, the man's mind is put at rest, he pokes his head from out of his hole and looks round; he takes a step, then two, like a mouse from La Fontaine,* then ventures all the way out from under his scaffold, then leaps onto it, repairs it, restores it, polishes it, strokes it, gets it working, makes it shine, begins to grease again the rusty old mechanism that is out of order from lack of use; all of a sudden he turns round, grabs the hair of one of the ill-fated wretches in the nearest prison who is expecting to live, drags him over, strips him of his wordly possessions, ties him up, fastens him down, and there you go: executions begin all over again.

All this is terrible, but it is part of history.

Yes, a six-month reprieve was granted to unfortunate prisoners whose punishment was gratuitously worsened by making them take up their lives again; then, for no reason, unnecessarily, without really knowing why, *for the pleasure of it*, one fine morning the reprieve was revoked and all these human beings were cold-bloodedly handed over to be systematically felled. My God! I ask you, what was it to us if these men lived? Isn't there enough air in France for us all to breathe?

For some mere clerk in the chancellery, who didn't feel strongly about it, to get up from his desk one day and say: "Well then! No one's thinking of abolishing the death penalty any more. It's time to start guillotining again!" – something quite monstrous must have happened deep down inside that man.

And to be frank, never had executions taken place in more appalling conditions than since the revoking of reprieves in July, never had stories from La Grève been more disgusting or greater justification for loathing the death penalty. This even greater wave of horror was just punishment for the men who reinstigated the law of blood. May they be punished by their own work. It serves them right.

Here I should give two or three examples of what was appalling and ungodly about some executions. We have to upset the crown prosecutors' wives. A wife is sometimes a conscience.

In the Midi, towards the end of last September, we can't quite remember the place, the day, or the condemned man's name, but if you disagree we can get the details – we think it was at Pamiers.* Anyway, around the end of September they come and get a man in prison where he was peacefully playing cards; they inform him he is to die in two hours' time, which sets him shaking all over, because for the last six months he had been forgotten, he wasn't expecting death any more; they shave him, cut his hair, tie him up, hear his confession, then cart him off through the crowd between four policemen to the place of execution. So far so good. That's the way it's done. At the scaffold, the executioner takes him over to the priest, brings him back, ties him to the bascule, *shoves him in the oven* to use the popular expression, and then releases the blade. The heavy iron triangle barely moves, it jolts down its runners, and now the horror starts, it gashes the man open without killing him. The man gives a terrible scream. Disconcerted, the executioner raises the blade and lets it drop again. The blade bites into the sufferer's neck a second time but still doesn't sever it. The sufferer howls, the crowd as well. The executioner hauls the blade up yet again, hoping for the best with the third go. No good. The third blow sends a third stream of blood spurting from the condemned man's neck but doesn't take his head off. To get to the point: the cutter rose and fell five times, five times it bit into the condemned man, five times the condemned man shrieked from the blow and shook his still-living head, begging for mercy! Infuriated, the people picked up stones and exercised their right by stoning the wretched headsman. The executioner took refuge under the guillotine and hid behind the police horses. But we aren't finished yet. Finding he was alone on the scaffold the victim got up from the plank and there, upright, horrifying, streaming with blood, supporting his half-removed head which was dangling on his shoulders, with feeble cries he asked for it to be cut off. The crowd, filled with pity, were about to force their way past the police to help this wretch who had been subjected to the death sentence five times over. At this point one of the executioner's assistants, a young man of twenty, climbs onto the scaffold, tells the sufferer to turn round so he can untie him and, taking advantage of the position of the dying man who was surrendering himself unsuspectingly, leaps onto his back and starts to cut through what was left of his neck with a butcher's knife. It happened. It was witnessed. Yes.

According to the law, a judge should have been present at the execution. He could have stopped everything with a sign. So what was this man doing inside his coach while they butchered another man? What was this punisher of murderers doing while they committed murder in broad daylight, under his nose, under his horses' noses, under the window of his carriage?

And the judge was not judged! The executioner was not judged! No court investigated this effacement of every law concerning the sacred person of one of God's creatures!

In the seventeenth century, that barbaric age of the *code criminel* under Richelieu, under Christophe Fouquet, when Monsieur de Chalais was put to death outside Le Bouffay prison in Nantes by a clumsy soldier who, instead of a single sword blow gave him thirty-four* with a cooper's axe, at least the parliament in Paris found it irregular; there was an enquiry and a trial, and if Richelieu was not punished, if Christophe Fouquet was not punished, the soldier was. No doubt unjust, but there was justice at the base of it.

But here, none. This thing took place after July, a time of progress and gentle mores, a year after the famous lament in the Chamber about the death penalty. Well! The event passed quite unnoticed. The Paris press reported it as trivia. No one had been alarmed. All they knew was that the guillotine had been deliberately tampered with by someone *who wanted to harm the enforcer of honourable works.** It was an executioner's assistant who, thrown out by his master, had taken revenge by playing a spiteful trick on him.

It was just a prank. Let's continue.

Three months ago in Dijon they executed a woman. (A woman!) Dr Guillotin's blade failed to do its job properly this time as well. The head wasn't completely cut off. So the enforcer's assistants grabbed hold of the woman's feet and, to the accompaniment of the poor devil's screams, they tugged and jerked the head from her body.

In Paris we have gone back to covert executions. Since they have not dared do any beheading at La Grève since July, since they are frightened, since they are cowards, this is what they do. They took a man from Bicêtre* recently, a condemned man – I think his name was Désandrieux – they put him in a sort of basket on two wheels, completely sealed, locked and padlocked; then with a policemen in front and a policeman at the rear, with little fuss and no crowds they delivered the package to the deserted toll gate at Saint-Jacques. When they arrived it was eight in the morning, barely daylight, there was a brand new guillotine set up and, for an audience, about a dozen little boys gathered on piles of stone round the unexpected apparatus; they quickly pulled him out of the basket and, without giving him time to draw breath, furtively, slyly, shamefully they had his head off. This is what goes by the name of a solemn public act of high justice. Unspeakable mockery!

So how do magistrates understand the word civilization? Where do we stand with it? Justice reduced to subterfuge and trickery! The law to machinations! Appalling!

It is an utterly dreadful thing for society to take a condemned man and treat him like that!

But to be fair the execution was not a total secret. That morning they proclaimed the death sentence at every crossroads in Paris and sold copies as usual. Apparently there are people who make a living from selling them. Do you hear? They turn some hapless individual's crime, his punishment, his torments, his death throes into a commodity, a piece of paper they sell for a sou. Can you imagine anything more repulsive than that sou, smothered in blood? And who pockets it?

Enough facts. More than enough. Isn't all this terrible? What excuse can you find for the death penalty?

We are asking a serious question; we are asking it in order to get an answer; we are asking criminal lawyers, not the chattering classes. We know there are people who find the pre-eminence of the death penalty a fascinating subject to study, just like any other. There are others who only like the death penalty because they hate someone who challenges it. For them it is almost a literary question, a question of personalities, proper names. These are envious people who no more find fault with legal experts than they do with great artists. The Filangieris aren't short of Joseph Grippas any more than Michelangelos are short of Torregianos, or Corneilles of Scudérys.*

It is not them we are talking to but the lawyers proper, the philosophical debaters, the thinkers, those who love the death penalty for the death penalty, for its beauty, its kindness, its mercy.

So let's hear their reasons.

Those who judge and pass sentence say the death penalty is necessary. Firstly because it is important to remove from the social body a member that has harmed it once and might harm it again. If it were simply a question of that, then life imprisonment would be sufficient. What use does death serve? You argue that people can escape from prison. You had better go and take a look at one. If you think the iron bars are not strong enough then how come you have zoos?

No need for an executioner when there is a jailer.

But let's continue. Society must take revenge, punish. It is neither one nor the other. Revenge is for the individual, punishment for God.

Society falls between the two. Punishment is above it, vengeance beneath. Neither something so great nor something so small befits it. It should not "punish to take revenge": it should correct in order to improve. Change the criminal lawyers' terminology to that and we will understand it, we will subscribe to it.

Which leaves the third and final reason, the theory of example. We have to set an example! We have to terrify with the sight of what fate has in store for criminals those who would be tempted to imitate them! There you have it! Almost word for word, the eternal phrase of which every summing-up speech for the prosecution in the five hundred public prosecutor's departments in France is just more or less another high-sounding variation. Well! Firstly we refuse to accept that it acts as an example. We refuse to accept that the sight of executions has the effect you think. Far from edifying people it demoralizes them, destroys any higher feelings they have, and consequently any morals. There is plenty of evidence, although it would get in the way of our argument to quote it. Nonetheless we will quote one incident among thousands, because it is the most recent. At the time of writing it was just ten days ago. It was on 5th March, the last day of carnival. At Saint-Pol, straight after the execution of an arsonist called Louis Camus, a group of people wearing masks danced round the still-steaming scaffold. So, make examples. The Mardi Gras laughs in your face.

But if despite experience you stick to your usual theory of example, then let's bring back the sixteenth century, that would be marvellous; bring back Farinacci,* bring back torturer-jurors; bring back the gallows, the wheel, the stake, the strappado, cutting off ears, quartering, burying alive, boiling alive; bring back the executioner's monstrous stall at every crossroads in Paris, continually stocked with fresh meat, just one more shop among the rest. Bring back Montfaucon,* its sixteen stone pillars, its crude assizes, its cellar filled with bones, its beams, its hooks, its chains, its rows of skeletons, its plaster knoll dotted with crows, its branched gibbets and the smell of corpses which the north-east wind carries in great gusts across the Faubourg du Temple. Bring back the Paris executioner's gigantic shed in all its permanence and power. There's a fine idea! There's an example on a grand scale. There's the death penalty and no mistake. There's a system of execution with a bit of proportion. There's something which is horrible, no, dreadful.

Or do what they do in England. In England, that mercantile nation, they catch a smuggler on the coast at Dover, they hang him as an example; as an example they leave him on the gallows; but since the inclement weather might damage the corpse they carefully wrap it in canvas smeared with tar so as not to have to replace it so often. O land of thrift! Tarring the hanged!

Yet it has logic. It is the most humane way to view the theory of example.

But you, do you seriously think you are making an example when you slit the throat of some poor man wretchedly and in the most deserted recesses of the outer boulevards? At La Grève in broad daylight is one thing; but at the gates of Saint-Jacques! At eight o'clock in the morning! Who will come past? Who will be going that way? Who knows you are killing a man there? Who is going to think you are setting an example? An example to whom? To the trees on the boulevard apparently.

So can't you see your public executions are being done on the sly? Can't you see you are hiding? That you are afraid, ashamed of your deeds? That you are absurd, spluttering your *discite justitiam moniti*?* That deep down you are shaken, unsettled, anxious, uncertain of being right, filled with doubts, cutting off heads as a matter of course without really knowing what you are doing? Deep down do you not at least feel you have lost the moral and social awareness of the bloody mission that your predecessors, those old members of parliament, carried out with such a clear conscience? Do you not you toss and turn in bed at night more than they did? Others before you ordered people to be executed, but they considered what they were doing to be right, just, good. Jouvenel des Ursins thought he was a judge; Élie de Thorrette thought he was a judge; Laubardement, La Reynie and Laffemas* thought they were judges; but in your heart of hearts you are never quite sure that you aren't murderers!

You forsake La Grève for the gates of Saint-Jacques, the crowd for isolation, daylight for twilight. You are not doing things with firmness any more. You are hiding, I tell you!

So all the reasons for the death penalty are demolished. All the public prosecutor's syllogisms are brought to naught. All these wood shavings of summings-up are swept away, reduced to ashes. The slightest contact with logic makes all false arguments disintegrate.

Just let the magistrates come asking us for heads again, us members of the jury, us men, imploring us in a cajoling voice in the name of protecting society, maintaining public convictions, making examples. It's all rhetoric, pomposity and emptiness! One pinprick in their grandiloquence and it deflates. Beneath their honeyed verbosity you just find hard-heartedness, cruelty, barbarity, the desire to demonstrate their zeal, the need to earn fees. Silence, mandarins! Under the judge's velvet glove we feel the claws of the executioner.

It is difficult to think calmly about what a criminal crown prosecutor is. He is a man who earns a living by sending others to the scaffold. He is the official purveyor to every Place de Grève. Not only that, he is a gentlemen with pretensions to style and literature, a fine speaker, or thinks he is, who if needs be will trot out a line or two of Latin before deciding on death, who tries to create an impression, who is fascinating to his personal sense of self-esteem – O woe! – who, where other people's lives are at stake, has his models, his appalling examples to live up to, his classics, his Bellart, his Marchangy,* like one poet has Racine and another Boileau. During the proceedings he fights on the guillotine's side; it is his role, his profession. His summing-up is his work of literature, he decks it with metaphors, perfumes it with quotations; it has to be good for the audience, it has to appeal to the ladies. He has his stock of commonplaces that are still brand new to provincials, his ornamental turns of phrase, his affectations, his writerly refinements. He hates the simple word almost as much as the tragic poets of the school of Delille. Have no fear he will call things by their proper name. Bah! For each idea which would disgust you in its naked form, he has disguises complete with epithets and adjectives. He makes Monsieur Sanson* presentable. He veils the blade. He blurs the bascule. He wraps the red basket in circumlocutions. You don't know where you are any more. Everything is rose-tinted and respectable. Can you picture him at night in his study, at leisure, doing his best to work up the harangue that in six weeks' time will have a scaffold built? Do you see him sweating blood to make the defendant's head fit into the deadliest article of the criminal code? Do you see him sawing through a poor wretch's neck with a badly made law? Do you see how he injects two or three poisonous passages into a muddle of tropes and synecdoches so that, with much ado, he can squeeze out, extract the death of a man from it? Is it not true that under the desk as he writes he probably has the executioner crouching at his feet in the shadows, and that he puts down his pen now and then to say to him, like a master to his dog: "Hush! Quiet now! You'll get your bone!"

What's more, in his private life this public servant might be a decent man, a good father, a good son, a good husband, a good friend – like it says on all the headstones in Père-Lachaise.

Let us hope the day is coming when the law will abolish these doleful duties. At some point the very air of our civilization must wear out the death penalty.

One is sometimes tempted to think that supporters of the death penalty have never really thought about it. But just weigh in the balance, against some crime or other, this outrageous right that society assumes to take away something it did not give, this punishment, the most irreversible of all irreversible punishments.

There are two possibilities:

Either the man you strike down has no family, no relatives, no one he is attached to in the world. In which case he has had no education, no upbringing, no one to take care of his mind or his feelings; so by what right do you kill this miserable orphan? You are punishing him for a childhood that crept along the ground as it grew, without stem or stake! The offence you accuse him of is the isolation to which you abandoned him! You turn his misfortune into his crime! No one taught him to know what he was doing. This man doesn't know. It is not him who is the owner of his misdeed – his fate is. You are striking down an innocent.

Or the man has a family; so do you think the blow with which you cut his throat will hurt just him? That his father, his mother, his children will not bleed because of it? No. By killing him you decapitate his entire family. And again you strike down the innocent.

Blind and clumsy penalty which strikes the innocent whichever way it turns.

This man, this guilty man with a family, lock him away. In prison he will still be able to work for his loved ones. But how will he provide for them from the grave? Can you think without shuddering about what will become of the little boys, the little girls whose father you have taken, in other words their bread? In fifteen years' time, will you be depending on the men of this family to supply the penal colony, the women the common dance hall? Oh! Poor innocents!

In the colonies, when a slave is executed by warrant the man's owner gets a thousand francs' compensation. What! You reimburse the master but not the family! Here too are you not taking a man from those he belongs to? Is he not, in a sacred way quite different from that of a slave in relation to his master, his father's property, his wife's possession, his children's asset?

We have already convicted your law of murder. Now it is convicted of theft.

And another thing. Do you stop to think of this man's soul? Do you know what state it is in? Do you dare dispose of it so lightly? At least in the past the people had some faith; at the hour of reckoning the breath of religion in the air could soften the most hardened heart;

a sufferer was also a penitent; the moment society closed one door on him, religion opened another; every soul was conscious of God; the scaffold was merely the gateway to heaven. But what hopes can you place on the scaffold now the masses no longer believe, now all religions are riddled with dry rot like those old ships that languish in our ports, yet which long ago may have discovered new worlds? Now that children poke fun at God? By what right do you cast the darkened souls of the condemned, souls such as Voltaire and Monsieur Pigault-Lebrun* created, into a place whose existence you yourselves question? You hand them over to your prison chaplain – without doubt a splendid old man, but does he believe and inspire belief? Does he not make a meal of his exalted task as if it were a chore? Do you take him for a priest, this fellow who rubs shoulders with the headsman in the tumbril? A talented and noble writer has already said: "It is a terrible thing to keep the executioner after you have dispensed with the confessor."

These are probably just "sentimental reasons", as scornful people call them, whose logic comes only from their heads. In our eyes they are the best. We often prefer reasons of sentiment to reasons of reasoning. And anyway, let's not forget that these two trains of thought are connected. *On Crimes and Punishments* is an offshoot of *On the Spirit of the Laws*. Montesquieu fathered Beccaria.

Reason is on our side, feelings are on our side, experience is on our side as well. In model states, where the death penalty has been abolished, the number of capital offences goes down progessively each year. Give that some thought.

However, for the moment we are not asking for a sudden and total abolition of the death penalty, like the Chamber of Deputies so rashly committed themselves to. On the contrary, what we would like is every sensible attempt, precaution, tentative step. Besides, we do not just want the death penalty abolished, we want a complete revision of all forms of punishment from top to bottom, from prison bars to the blade, and time is one of the elements that must be included in such an undertaking if it is to be done properly. We also intend to develop what we feel is the relevant conceptual approach to this subject. But over and above partial abolitions for forgery, arson, aggravated theft, etc., we ask that from now on, in every capital case the judge should have to put this question to the jury: "Did the defendant act out of passion or self-interest?" And if the jury reply: "The defendant acted out of passion," there should be no death sentence. This would spare us a few atrocious executions at least. Ulbach and Debacker would be saved. We would no longer guillotine Othello.

What's more, and let us not deceive ourselves, the matter of the death penalty evolves every day. It will not be long before the whole of society is of the same mind as us.

The criminal lawyers had best take heed, the death penalty has been declining for a century. It has almost become gentle. A sign of decay. A sign of weakness. A sign of approaching death. Torture has disappeared. The wheel has disappeared. The gallows has disappeared. What a strange thing! The guillotine is a form of progress.

Monsieur Guillotin was a philanthropist.

Yes, the hideous, toothed, ravening Themis of Farinacci and Vouglans, of Delancre and Isaac Loisel, of Oppède and Machault* is wasting away. She is getting thinner. She is dying.

Already La Grève wants no more to do with it. La Grève is changing her image. The old bloodsucker behaved herself in July. She wants to lead a better life from now on, be worthy of her last good deed. She who prostituted herself to every scaffold for three hundred years has come over bashful. She is ashamed of her former profession. She wants to lose her bad name. She renounces the headsman. She is washing down her paving stones.

Even now the death penalty has moved out of Paris. And let us say this here, to leave Paris is to leave civilization.

All the indications are on our side. It seems, too, that this repulsive machine, or rather that monster made of wood and steel that is to Guillotin what Galatea was to Pygmalion, is discouraged, baulking. In some ways the horrifying executions we described earlier are a good sign. The guillotine is hesitating. It misses its target. All the old apparatus of the death penalty is breaking down.

This vile machine will leave France, we are counting on it, and God willing it will leave with a limp, because we will make sure to give it a few hefty blows.

Let it seek hospitality elsewhere, from some barbaric race, but not Turkey, which is becoming civilized, not from the savages,* who wouldn't have it; let it go down a few more rungs on the ladder of civilization, to Spain or Russia.

The social structure of the past rested on three pillars: the priest, the king, the executioner. It is a long time now since a voice said: "The gods are dying!" Recently another voice cried out: "The kings are dying!" Now it is time for another voice to say: "The executioner is dying!"

Thus the old society will vanish stone by stone, and in this way destiny will complete the collapse of the past.

To those who missed the gods we could say: there is always God. To those who miss the King we can say: there is always the homeland. To those who will miss the executioner we have nothing to say.

But public order will not disappear along with the executioner; never believe that. The vault of future society will not collapse for lack of that one monstrous keystone. Civilization is no more than a series of transformations. So what is it you are about to witness? The transformation of the system of punishment. The gentle law of Christ will finally penetrate the penal code and extend its influence across it. Crime will be seen as a disease, and this disease will have doctors instead of judges, hospitals instead of penal colonies. Liberty and health will be the same thing. Balm and oil will be poured on where once steel and fire were applied. The evil that was treated with anger will be treated with charity. It will be simple and sublime. The cross in place of the gallows. That is all.

15th March 1832

A Comedy about a Tragedy*

Dramatis Personae

Madame de Blinval
The Chevalier
Ergaste
An elegiac poet
A philosopher
A fat gentleman
A thin gentleman
Women
A footman

A salon

AN ELEGIAC POET: (*reading*)

> "...*The next day, through the forest a-heading,*
> *A dog roamed the riverbank a-barking;*
> *And when the gracious young girl, in tears*
> *Sat down once again, her heart full of fears,*
> *On the old old tower of the ancient châtel,*
> *She heard the moans of the water, sad Isaura,*
> *But no longer the mandora*
> *Of the sweet minstrel!*"

THE WHOLE COMPANY: Bravo! Charming! Delightful!

(*They clap their hands.*)

MADAME DE BLINVAL: There's an inexpressible mystery in the ending that brings tears to the eyes.

ELEGIAC POET: (*modestly*) The catastrophe is concealed.

THE CHEVALIER: (*nodding*) "Mandora", "minstrel", that's so romantic!

ELEGIAC POET: Yes Monsieur, but reasonable romanticism, true romanticism. What do you expect? One has to make a few allowances.

CHEVALIER: Allowances! Allowances! That's how one loses one's sense of taste. I'd give all the romantic poetry in the world for this one quatrain:

> "*From Kythira and Pindus,*
> *Sweet Bernard word did receive*

> *That the Art of Love on Saturday eve*
> *Must dine with the Art to Please."*

That's real poetry! "The Art of Love dining on Saturday with the Art to Please!" It's frightfully good! But nowadays it's "the mandora", "the minstrel". They don't write *ephemeral poetry* any more. If I were a poet I would write *ephemeral poetry*; but I'm not a poet.

ELEGIAC POET: Nonetheless, elegies…

CHEVALIER: *Ephemeral poetry*, Monsieur. (*Aside to Madame de Blinval:*) And anyway, *châtel* isn't French; we say *castel*.

SOMEONE: (*to the elegiac poet:*) An observation, Monsieur. You say "ancient châtel", why not "Gothic"?

ELEGIAC POET: One doesn't say *Gothic* in verse.

SOMEONE: Ah! So it's different.

ELEGIAC POET: (*continuing*) So you see, Monsieur, one has to know one's limits. I'm not one of those who wants to play havoc with French verse and take us back to the time of the Ronsards and the Brébeufs. I'm a Romantic, but restrained. It's the same with emotions. I prefer them gentle, dreamy, melancholy, no blood, no horrors. Conceal the catastrophe. I know there are some people, madmen, frenzied imaginations that… I say, ladies, have you read that new novel?

LADIES: Which novel?

ELEGIAC POET: *The Last Day…*

A FAT GENTLEMAN: Enough, Monsieur! I know the one you mean. The title alone troubles my nerves.

MADAME DE BLINVAL: Mine too. It's a ghastly book. I have it here.

LADIES: Let us see. (*The book is passed round.*)

SOMEONE: (*reading*) *The Last day of...*

FAT GENTLEMAN: Madame, I beg you!

MADAME DE BLINVAL: It really is an appalling book, a book that gives one nightmares, a book that makes one ill.

A WOMAN: (*aside*) I must read it.

FAT GENTLEMAN: It must be said that morals deteriorate every day. My Lord, what a horrible thought! To uncover, dig up, analyse one by one without overlooking a single one, every physical suffering, every mental torment that a man condemned to death must feel on the day of his execution! Isn't it appalling? Can you imagine it ladies, there was a writer to have this idea and members of the public to read this writer?

CHEVALIER: Indeed, it's monumentally impertinent.

MADAME DE BLINVAL: Who is the author?

FAT GENTLEMAN: There wasn't a name on the first edition.

ELEGIAC POET: It's the one who has already written two other novels... goodness, I've forgotten their titles. The first one begins in the Morgue and ends at La Grève. In every chapter there's an ogre who eats a child.

FAT GENTLEMAN: You've read it, Monsieur?

ELEGIAC POET: Yes, Monsieur; it's set in Iceland.

FAT GENTLEMAN: Iceland, that's awful!

ELEGIAC POET: What's more he's written odes, ballads or whatever, where there are monsters with *blue bodies*.

CHEVALIER: (*laughing*) Odds bodkins!* That must make a ripping poem.

ELEGIAC POET: He has also published a play – they call it a play – in which there is this handsome line:

"*Tomorrow the twenty-fifth of June sixteen hundred and fifty-seven.*"*

SOMEONE: Ah, that line!

ELEGIAC POET: Although it could be written in figures, you see, ladies:

"*Tomorrow, 25th June 1657.*"

(*He laughs. They laugh.*)

CHEVALIER: It's quite particular, poetry these days.

FAT GENTLEMAN: Absolutely! He can't write verse, this man! What's his name, actually?

ELEGIAC POET: His name is as hard to remember as it is to pronounce. There's something of the Goth, the Visigoth, the Ostrogoth in it. (*He laughs.*)

MADAME DE BLINVAL: He's a nasty man.

FAT GENTLEMAN: A frightful man.

A YOUNG WOMAN: Someone who knows him told me—

FAT GENTLEMAN: You know someone who knows him?

YOUNG WOMAN: Yes, they say he's a gentle man, simple, who lives quietly and spends all day playing with his children.

ELEGIAC POET: And all night dreaming up works of darkness... it's remarkable – that line just came to me. But that's what poetry is:

"And all night dreaming up works of darkness."

With a good caesura. There's just the other rhyme to find. By Jove!
– *starkness.*

MADAME DE BLINVAL: *"Quidquid tentabat dicere, versus erat".* *

FAT GENTLEMAN: So you're saying the author in question has small
children? Impossible, madame. When he wrote that book! A
dreadful novel!

SOMEONE: But why did he write it, this novel?

ELEGIAC POET: How should I know?

A PHILOSOPHER: To campaign for the abolition of the death penalty
apparently.

FAT GENTLEMAN: A horror, I tell you!

CHEVALIER: Absolutely! So it's a duel with the executioner?

ELEGIAC POET: He has a frightful grudge against the guillotine.

A THIN GENTLEMAN: I can see that from here. It's nothing but ranting.

FAT GENTLEMAN: Exactly. There are barely two pages about the death
penalty in this text. All the rest is sensationalism.

PHILOSOPHER: That's the problem. The subject merits logical discussion.
A play, a novel, proves nothing. And besides I've read the book, it's
no good.

ELEGIAC POET: Atrocious. Is that art? It's going too far, it's putting the
cat among the pigeons. And this murderer, do I know him? Not
at all. What has he done? We have no idea. He might be a really
bad sort. People have no right to concern me with someone I don't
know.

FAT GENTLEMAN: They have no right to make the reader suffer physically. When I watch tragedies, people kill each other. Fair enough! That doesn't bother me. But this novel makes your hair stand on end, makes your flesh creep. I spent two days in bed after reading it.

PHILOSOPHER: Added to which it's a cold, formal book.

ELEGIAC POET: A book!... A book!

PHILOSOPHER: Yes – and as you were just saying, Monsieur, there's no genuine aesthetic to it. I'm not interested in abstractions, flawless beings. I don't see any personality here in keeping with my own. And anyway, the style is neither clear nor simple. It smacks of archaism. That's exactly what you were saying, isn't it?

ELEGIAC POET: Undoubtedly, undoubtedly. There's no need for personalities.

PHILOSOPHER: The condemned man isn't interesting.

ELEGIAC POET: How could he be interesting? He has a crime but no feeling of remorse. I would have done quite the reverse. I would have told the story of my condemned man. The son of decent parents. A good education. Love. Jealousy. A crime that wasn't really a crime. And then remorse, remorse, lots of remorse. But the law is unbending: he has to die. That's how I would have treated the question of the death penalty. Yes, a fine idea!

MADAME DE BLINVAL: Ah! Ah!

PHILOSOPHER: Forgive me, but the book Monsieur intends to write wouldn't prove a thing. The specific case doesn't govern the majority.

ELEGIAC POET: Well, even better! For the hero why not choose... Malesherbes, for example, the righteous Malesherbes? His last day, his execution? Oh, such a fine and noble sight! I would have wept, I would have trembled, I would have wanted to mount the scaffold with him.

PHILOSOPHER: I wouldn't.

CHEVALIER: Me neither. He was a revolutionary at heart, your Monsieur de Malesherbes.

PHILOSOPHER: The execution of Malesherbes doesn't prove anything against the death penalty in general.

FAT GENTLEMAN: The death penalty! What's the point of getting involved with that? What's it to you, the death penalty? This author must be thoroughly low-born to go giving us nightmares about it with this book of his.

MADAME DE BLINVAL: Oh, yes! So very unfeeling!

FAT GENTLEMAN: He makes us look at prisons, penal colonies, at Bicêtre. It's most unpleasant. We know perfectly well they're cesspits. But what does it matter to society?

MADAME DE BLINVAL: The people who made the laws weren't children.

PHILOSOPHER: Ah, but still! By showing things in their true light...

THIN GENTLEMAN: I'm afraid that's exactly what's missing, the truth. How can you expect a poet to know anything about such matters? You would have to be a crown prosecutor at least. Look: I read an extract from this book in a newspaper, and in it, when they read out his death sentence the condemned man says nothing; well, I've seen a condemned man at that moment, and he gave a great cry. So you see.

PHILOSOPHER: If I may...

THIN GENTLEMAN: Look, Messieurs, the guillotine, La Grève, that's all in poor taste. And what proves it is that it's apparently a book that corrupts one's taste and makes one incapable of pure, fresh, innocent feelings. And when are the champions of wholesome literature going to rise up? I'd like to be – and my summings-up for the prosecution might make me eligible – a member of the Académie Française ... But here's Monsieur Ergaste, who is. What does he think of *The Last Day of a Condemned Man*?

ERGASTE: Well, Monsieur, I've neither read it nor will I. I had dinner with Madame de Sénange yesterday, and the Marquise de Morival was talking about it to the Duc de Melcour. They say it has characters who are against the magistrature, and especially Judge d'Alimont. The Abbé de Floricour was offended as well. Apparently it has a chapter against religion and a chapter against the monarchy. If I were a crown prosecutor!...

CHEVALIER: Oh well, yes, a crown prosecutor! And the charter! And the freedom of the press! Still, a poet who wants to get rid of the death penalty, you must agree it's unspeakable. Oh! Oh! Under the Ancien Régime, someone who dared publish a novel against torture!... But since the storming of the Bastille you can write anything. Books do terrible harm.

FAT GENTLEMAN: Terrible. We used to be quite peaceful, there was nothing to think about. From time to time they cut a head off here and there in France, two a week at most. All without fuss, without any outcry. They never said a word. Nobody stopped to think about it. Not at all. And then along comes a book... a book that gives you a ghastly headache!

THIN GENTLEMAN: What could a member of a jury do after reading it but convict!

ERGASTE: It troubles people's consciences.

MADAME DE BLINVAL: Oh! Books! Books! Who would have thought it of a novel?

ELEGIAC POET: It's true that books often act as a subversive poison on the social order.

THIN GENTLEMAN: Not to mention language, which those gentlemen the Romantics are revolutionizing too.

ELEGIAC POET: We must make a distinction, Monsieur; there are Romantics and Romantics.

THIN GENTLEMAN: Poor taste, poor taste.

ERGASTE: You are right. Poor taste.

THIN GENTLEMAN: There's no answer to that.

PHILOSOPHER: (*leaning on a lady's chair*) They say things in them that people don't even say in the Rue Mouffetard any more.

ERGASTE: Oh! That frightful book!

MADAME DE BLINVAL: I say, don't throw it on the fire! It's on loan from the library.

CHEVALIER: Tell me about our day. How everything has degenerated since then, people's taste, their behaviour! Do you remember what it was like in our day, Madame de Blinval?

MADAME DE BLINVAL: No, Monsieur, I don't.

CHEVALIER: We were the gentlest, happiest, wittiest people. Always fine parties, lovely poetry. It was delightful. What could be more gallant than the madrigal Monsieur de la Harpe wrote about the grand ball that Madame la Maréchale de Mailly threw in seventeen hundred... the year they executed Damiens?*

FAT GENTLEMAN: (*sighs*) Happy days! But nowadays the behaviour is terrible, as well as the books. It's like that beautiful line by Boileau:

*"And the fall of art follows the decline of behaviour."**

PHILOSOPHER: (*aside to the poet*) Do we get fed in this house?

ELEGIAC POET: Yes, in just a moment.

THIN GENTLEMAN: Now they want to abolish the death penalty, and so they write brutal, immoral novels in bad taste, *The Last Day of a Condemned Man*, whatever next?

FAT GENTLEMAN: Look, my dear fellow, we mustn't talk about that frightful book any more – and tell me, since I've run into you, what are you doing about that man whose appeal we rejected three weeks ago?

THIN GENTLEMAN: Oh, hang on! I'm on leave at the moment. Give me time to breath. I'll see when I get back. But if it's still taking too long I'll write to my deputy.

FOOTMAN: (*entering*) Dinner is served.

The Last Day of
a Condemned Man

1

CONDEMNED TO DEATH!
I have been living with this thought for five weeks now, always alone with it, always chilled by its presence, always bent under its weight!

Once, because it seems years rather than weeks, I was a man like other men. Every day, every hour, every minute had its idea. My mind, young and fertile, was full of fancies. It liked to lay them out in front of me one by one, non-stop and at random, embellishing the crude and flimsy stuff of life with a never-ending stream of ornaments. There were young girls, bishops' magnificent copes, battles won, theatres full of noise and light, and then more young girls, walks in the dark of night beneath the spreading arms of the chestnut trees. There was always a party going on in my imagination. I could think about whatever I liked, I was free.

Now I'm a prisoner. My body is in irons in a dungeon, my mind imprisoned in an idea. A terrible, bloody, remorseless idea! I have only one thought now, one belief, one certainty: condemned to death!

Whatever I do this hellish thought is always there, like a leaden ghost beside me, alone and jealous, driving all other distractions away, face to face with wretched me, shaking me with its icy hands whenever I try and turn away or close my eyes. It creeps in everywhere my mind would like to escape to, mingles with every word that's spoken to me like an awful chorus, presses itself against the bars of my dungeon with me; haunts my waking, spies on my spasmodic sleep, appears in my dreams in the shape of a blade.

I have just woken with a start, hounded by it, thinking: "Oh, it's just a dream!" But no! Before my heavy eyelids have had time to open wide enough to see the deadly reality that surrounds me on the damp, dripping flagstones of my cell, in the pale glimmer of light from my lamp, in the coarse weave of my rough canvas clothes, on the stern face of the sentry whose cartridge pouch glints through the bars of my dungeon, it seems as if a voice has already whispered in my ear: "Condemned to death!"

2

I T WAS ON A FINE MORNING IN AUGUST.
It was three days since my trial had begun, three days that my name and crime had been drawing hordes of onlookers who swept down onto the benches of the courtroom like crows round a corpse, three days that the fantastical band of judges, witnesses, lawyers, crown prosecutors had passed back and forth in front of me, now grotesque, now bloody, always grim and deadly. The first two nights I couldn't sleep from anxiety and dread; on the third I slept from boredom and fatigue. At midnight I left the jury deliberating. I was taken back to the straw in my dungeon and straight away fell into a deep sleep, a sleep of oblivion. It was the first rest I had had for many days.

I was still at the deepest point of that deep sleep when they came to wake me. This time the heavy tread and hobnailed boots of the deputy jailer, the jangling of his keys, the harsh grating of the bolts was not enough; it took his rough voice in my ear, his rough hand on my arm to drag me from listlessness – "Get up then!" I opened my eyes, sat up in alarm. At that instant, through the high narrow window of the cell I saw, on the ceiling of the corridor outside, the only sky it was given me to see, that yellowish play of light by which eyes grown accustomed to the gloom of prison immediately recognize the sun. I love the sun.

"Nice weather," I said to the jailer.

For a moment he didn't reply, as if unsure whether it was worth the cost of a word; then with some effort he muttered curtly:

"Maybe."

I didn't move, mind half-drowsy, mouth smiling, eyes fixed on the soft golden ripples that were mottling the ceiling.

"Looks like a nice day," I repeated.

"Yes," he replied. "They're waiting for you."

Those few words, like the thread that stops a fly in mid-flight, hurled me back to reality. As if in a flash of lightning I suddenly saw the dark courtroom, the horseshoe of judges weighed down with their blood-soaked rags, the three rows of witnesses with silly faces, the two policemen at each end of my bench, and the black gowns bustling about, the faces of the crowd thronging in the shadows at the back and, fastened on me, the fixed gaze of the twelve jurors who had stayed awake while I was asleep!

I got up; my teeth were chattering, my hands were shaking and couldn't find my clothes, my legs were weak. With my first step I stumbled like a porter with too much to carry. Yet I followed the jailer.

Two policemen were waiting outside the cell. They put the handcuffs back on me. They had a small, awkward little lock that they did up carefully. I let them: it was one machine working on another.

We went across an inner courtyard. The brisk morning air revived me. I looked up. The sky was blue and, interrupted by the tall chimneys, warm rays of sunlight traced patterns at the top of the tall dark walls of the prison. It was beautiful.

We went up a spiral staircase; we passed a corridor, then another, then a third; then a low door opened. A mixture of noise and warm air hit me in the face: it was the breath of the crowd in the courtroom. I went in.

As I appeared there was a mumble of weapons and voices. Benches were shifted noisily. Partitions creaked, and as I crossed the long room between the two blocs of the public behind walls of soldiers, it was as if I was the central point to which the strings that made all these gaping, straining faces move were attached.

At that moment I noticed I wasn't in irons, but I couldn't remember when they had been taken off.

Then there was silence. I reached my seat. The moment the commotion stopped among the crowd, it stopped in my mind too. And suddenly I understood clearly what up till then I had only made out confusedly, that the critical moment had arrived, that I was here to hear my sentence.

It's hard to explain, but the way the idea came to me didn't frighten me at all. The windows were open; the noises and the air of the town came in from outside; the room was bright as if for a wedding; here and there cheerful sunbeams traced the brilliant outline of the casements along the floor, across the tables, sometimes broken up in the corners; and from the dazzling diamond shapes of the windows each ray carved out a great prism of golden dust in the air.

At the far end the judges seemed satisfied, presumably delighted that they would soon be finished. In the presiding judge's face, lit up softly by a reflection from a window pane, there was something peaceful and kind; a young assessor, carefully rearranging his bands, was chatting away almost merrily with a pretty lady in a pink hat who had been given a seat behind him as a special favour.

Only the jury looked pale and exhausted, but it must have been from being up all night. Some of them were yawning. Nothing in their expressions gave any sign that these were men who had just handed down a death sentence; all I could make out on the faces of these good citizens was the desire to get some sleep.

Opposite me a window was wide open. I could hear the laughter of the flower sellers on the embankment; and on the edge of the window a pretty little yellow flower, filled with sun, danced in the breeze through a crack in the stone.

How could any gruesome thought find its way in through so many friendly sensations? Bathed in fresh air and sunlight it was impossible to think of anything but freedom; hope shone inside me like the daylight all around, and I waited confidently for my sentence just as you wait for liberation and life.

In the meantime my lawyer arrived. They had been waiting for him. He had just breakfasted well and heartily. Once he sat down he leant towards me and smiled.

"I'm hopeful," he said.

"Are you?" I replied, flippant and smiling too.

"Yes," he went on. "I don't know what the verdict is yet, but I expect they will have ruled out malice aforethought, so it will only be hard labour for life."

"What do you mean, Monsieur?" I replied, indignantly. "I'd rather it was death, a thousand times."

Yes, death! "Besides," some voice inside me said, "what risk is there in saying that? Have they ever passed the death sentence except at midnight, by torchlight in a dark dismal courtroom on a cold wet winter night? But in August, at eight o'clock in the morning on such a lovely day, with this good, kind jury, it's impossible!" And I went back to staring at the pretty yellow flower in the sunlight.

Suddenly the presiding judge, who had just been waiting for my lawyer, asked me to stand up. The soldiers shouldered arms; as if by electricity the whole room was on its feet at the same instant. An insignificant, almost non-existent figure sitting at a table below the bench – I think it was the clerk of the court – began to speak, and read out the verdict that the jury had given in my absence. A cold sweat broke out all over me; I leant on the wall so as not to fall over.

"Counsel for the defence, have you anything to say before I pass sentence?" the judge asked.

Personally I would have had a lot to say, but I couldn't think of anything. My tongue was stuck to the roof of my mouth.

My lawyer stood up.

I realized he was trying to mitigate the jury's verdict, and to submit, instead of the sentence that went with it, the other sentence, the one I had been so upset to see him hoping for.

My indignation must have been very great to show itself among the thousands of emotions that were competing for my thoughts. I wanted to repeat out loud what I'd already said: "I'd rather it was death, a thousand times." But I couldn't find the breath, all I could do was hold him back roughly by the arm and cry out uncontrollably: "No!"

The public prosecutor battled with my lawyer while I listened with bemused satisfaction. Then the judges went out, then came back in again, and the presiding judge read out my sentence.

"Condemned to death!" said the crowd, and as I was led away all the people came rushing after me with a sound like a building collapsing. I just walked, feeling drunk and dumbfounded. Revolution had broken out inside of me. Until the death sentence I could feel myself breathing, quivering, living in the same world as other men; now I could clearly make out something like a wall between the world and myself. Nothing seemed like before. The large light-filled windows, the beautiful sun, the clear sky, the pretty flower, they were all pale, white, the colour of a shroud. These men, these women, these children who crushed forwards as I went past, to me they were like ghosts.

At the bottom of the stairs a dirty black carriage with barred windows was waiting for me. As I climbed in I glanced round the square. "That one's condemned to death!" shouted passers-by, running towards the carriage. Through the cloud that seemed to have come between me and everything else I made out two young girls watching me avidly. "Oh goody," said the younger one, clapping her hands. "It'll be in six weeks' time!"

3

C ONDEMNED TO DEATH!
And why not? "All men," I remember reading in some book or other, of which this was the only good part, "all men are condemned to death with their sentence suspended indefinitely".* So what had actually changed for me?

Since the moment my death sentence was passed, how many people who had been planning to have a long life had died! How many of them, young and free and healthy, who had been intending to come and see my head roll on the Place de Grève had got there before me! Between now and then, how many people, walking around and breathing in the open air, coming and going as they liked, would still get there before me!

Besides, what was there about life that I would I actually miss? The dreary light, the black bread of the dungeon, my ration of thin soup squeezed from the convicts' stewpot, being roughly treated – me, someone civilized by education – manhandled by jailers and warders, not seeing another human being who thought me worth talking to and who I felt the same about, constantly shuddering about what I had done as well as what they were going to do to me – to be honest, those were about the only possessions the headsman could take from me.

Oh what does it matter, it's appalling!

4

T HE BLACK CARRIAGE BROUGHT ME HERE, to monstrous Bicêtre.
From a distance the building looks quite stately. It appears on the brow of a hill on the horizon, and from a way off retains some of its former grandeur, the semblance of a royal château. But the closer you get the more dilapidated the palace turns out to be. The rotting gables are painful to behold. I don't know what, but something disgraceful and degenerate sullies the regal façade; it's as if the walls have leprosy. No more windows, no more window panes; just solid criss-crossed iron bars to which here and there the gaunt face of a convict or a lunatic is pressed.

Here you see life in the raw.

5

No sooner had i arrived than firm hands seized hold of me. The precautions were stepped up: no knives, no forks for eating with; a straitjacket, a kind of sack made of sailcloth, gripped me tightly round the arms; they had my life to answer for. I had lodged an appeal. This costly business might go on for six or seven weeks and it was important to get me to the Place de Grève in one piece.

For the first few days I was treated with a gentleness that appalled me. Sympathy from a jailer smacks of the scaffold. Luckily, after a short while the usual routine took over; they mixed me up with the other prisoners in the collective brutality and stopped making unaccustomed kind exceptions that constantly reminded me of the executioner. It wasn't the only improvement. My youth, my submissiveness, the kind efforts of the prison chaplain and especially the few words of Latin I spoke to the prison supervisor, who didn't understand them, earned me a walk with the other prisoners once a week and rid me of the disabling straitjacket. After much hesitation I was also given ink, pen and paper and a small reading lamp.

Every Sunday after mass they let me out into the yard at exercise time. Here I can talk to the other prisoners; I really need that. They are good people, the poor wretches. They tell me about their dodges; it would horrify you, but I know they're bragging. They teach me the slang, to *rabbit the lingo* as they say. It's a whole language grafted onto everyday speech like a sort of hideous growth, a wart. Sometimes it has extraordinary force, an alarming and vivid irony: *there's strawberry jam on the frog* (blood on the road), *to marry the widow* (be hung) – as if the gallows rope was the widow of every hanged man. A thief's head has two names: *the sorbonne*, when it is contemplating, arguing about and encouraging a crime; *the crust* when the executioner cuts it off. Sometimes there is music-hall humour: *a wicker handkerchief* (a rag-and-bone man's pannier), *the liar* (the tongue); and everywhere, all the time, peculiar and mysterious words, ugly and squalid words that come from who knows where: *the stretch* (the executioner), *the cone* (death), *the shelf* (the place of execution). It makes you think of toads and spiders. When you hear people speak this language it's as if something dirty and dusty, a bundle of rags, is being shaken in your face.

At least these men pity me, but they're the only ones. The jailers, the deputy jailers, the turnkeys – I've nothing against them – laugh and gossip, talk about me, in front of me, as if I were just an object.

6*

I SAID TO MYSELF:
Since I have something to write with, why not do it? But what to write? Stuck between four cold, bare stone walls, with nowhere for my legs to take me, no horizon to look at, my only occupation being to spend all day mechanically watching the slow progress of the whitish square that the spyhole in my door projects onto the dark wall opposite and, as I was just saying, all alone with an idea, an idea of crime and punishment, of murder and death! Did I have anything to say, I who have nothing more to do in this world? And what is there in my empty withered brain worth writing about?

But why not? If everything around me is drab and colourless, isn't there a storm, a struggle, a tragedy going on inside me? Doesn't the obsession that has hold of me appear to me every hour, every second in a new form, more monstrous, more bloody the nearer the final day comes? Why don't I try and tell myself about all the violent, unfamiliar feelings I am having in this situation of abandonment? There is certainly no lack of material, and as short as my life may be there is still enough in the dread, the terror, the torments that are going to fill it from this moment till the last which can wear out a pen, run an inkwell dry. Besides, the only way not to suffer so much from this dread is to examine it; describing it will take my mind off it.

And anyway, maybe what I write won't be pointless. Won't this hour-by-hour, minute-by-minute, torture-by-torture diary of my sufferings, if I am strong enough to carry on until it becomes *physically* impossible to do so, this story of my feelings, by necessity unfinished although also as complete as possible, bring with it a great, profound lesson? In this statement of dying thoughts, this ever-growing sorrow, this form of mental post-mortem of a condemned man, is there not something for those who pass sentence to learn? Perhaps reading this will make them less flippant the next time it comes to tossing a thinking head, a man's head, onto what they call the scales of justice? Perhaps these poor devils have never stopped to think about the slow sequence of torment that the swift, efficient wording of the death sentence entails? Have they ever had a moment's pause at the heart-rending idea that inside the man whose head they are severing there is a mind; a mind that was expecting to live, a soul that wasn't the least prepared for death? No. All they see is the downwards motion of a triangular blade, and probably believe that for the condemned man there is nothing before or afterwards.

These sheets of paper will put them right. If they are perhaps published one day they will focus their attention on the sufferings of the mind for a moment; because these are the ones they are not aware of. They rejoice at being able to kill without causing the body almost any suffering. But that's just the problem! What is physical pain beside mental pain? For pity's sake, is that what laws are! The day will come, and maybe these memoirs, a wretch's last thoughts, will have played a part...

Unless the breeze bowls these muddy bits of paper around the prison yard after my death, or they get ruined in the rain and are used to paste over the cracks in a jailer's broken window.

7

WHY SHOULD WHAT I WRITE HERE be of use to others, stop judges from judging, spare unfortunates, innocent or guilty, the agony to which I have been condemned? What's the point? What does it matter? After my head has been cut off, what is it to me if they cut off other people's? Was I really stupid enough to think that? To tear down the scaffold after I've mounted it? What do I get out of it, I ask you?

What! The sun, the springtime, fields of flowers, birds singing in the morning, the clouds, the trees, nature, liberty, life – none of that is for me now!

Oh! It's me who needs saving! Can it really be true that it's not possible, that I have to die tomorrow, maybe today, that that's how it is? O God! The terrible thought of smashing your head against the cell wall!

8

I MUST COUNT UP what I have left:
Allow three days after the sentence was passed for my appeal to be lodged.

A week's delay at the public prosecutor's department of the Crown Court, after which the *papers*, as they call them, are sent to the minister.

Two weeks at the minister's office, who doesn't even know they exist, and yet who supposedly, after going through them, passes them on to the Court of Appeal. There they are filed, indexed, recorded – because there is a long queue for the guillotine and everyone has to wait his turn.

Two weeks to make sure you don't get preferential treatment.

Finally the court sits, usually on a Thursday, rejects twenty appeals at a stroke and sends them all back to the minister, who sends them back to the public prosecutor, who sends them back to the executioner. Three days.

On the morning of the fourth day, as he is tying his cravat, the deputy public prosecutor says to himself: "There's still that business to be settled." And so if the assistant clerk of the court doesn't have a luncheon with friends which will get in the way, the order for the execution is drafted, drawn up, a fair copy made, dispatched, and at dawn the next day the sound of a structure being hammered together is heard on the Place de Grève, while at every crossroads the town criers are yelling hoarsely at the top of their voices.

Six weeks in all. The young girl was right.

So it's at least five weeks now – maybe six, I daren't count – that I've been in this country cottage called Bicêtre, and I think Thursday was three days ago.

9

I HAVE JUST WRITTEN MY WILL.
What's the point? My sentence includes costs, and everything I own will barely cover it. The guillotine is expensive.

I leave a mother, I leave a wife, I leave a child.

A little three-year-old girl, sweet, rosy and delicate, with big black eyes and long chestnut hair.

She was two years and one month old the last time I saw her.

So after my death there will be three women, without a son, without a husband, without a father; three different kinds of orphan; three widows on account of the law.

I admit I'm being justly punished, but what have they done, these innocents? No matter: they will be disgraced, ruined. That's justice for you.

It's not that I'm worried about my poor old mother: she's sixty-four, it will kill her. Although if she keeps going a few days longer let's hope she has a bit of hot ash in her foot-warmer up till the last moment; she won't complain.

I'm not worried about my wife either: her health isn't good and she's feeble-minded. She'll die too.

Unless she goes mad. They say that that makes you live longer, but at least your mind doesn't suffer; she'll be asleep, it'll be just as if she were dead.

But my daughter, my child, my poor little Marie, who laughs, who plays, who at this very moment is singing without a care in the world, she is the one who is hurting me!

10

THIS IS WHAT MY DUNGEON CONSISTS OF:
Eight square feet. Four stone walls built on a flagstone floor a step's height above the corridor outside.

To the right of the door as you come in, a sort of recess that is laughingly called an alcove. They throw a bale of straw in it, where the prisoner is supposed to rest and sleep, wearing canvas trousers and a ticking jacket summer and winter alike.

Above my head, by way of sky, a black *rib* vault – that's what it's called – from which thick spiders' webs dangle like rags.

No windows, not even a small one at floor level. A door covered in so much steel that you can't see the wood.

I'm wrong: in the middle of the door, near the top, a nine-inch square opening covered with a grille, and which the deputy jailer can close at night.

Outside, a fairly long corridor made light and airy by tiny narrow windows high up on the walls, and divided into brick bays connected by a series of low, arched doors; each bay acts as a form of anteroom to a dungeon similar to mine. These dungeons are where they put convicts whom the prison governor has had clapped in irons. The first three cells are reserved for those condemned to death; being closer to the jail they are more convenient for the jailer.

The dungeons are all that remain of the old Château de Bicêtre, built in the fifteenth century by the Cardinal of Winchester, the one who had Joan of Arc burnt at the stake. I heard this from some of the *curious* who came to see me in my room the other day, and who looked at me from a distance like an animal in a zoo. The deputy jailer made a hundred sous out of it.

I forgot to say there is a sentry on duty outside my dungeon night and day, and I can never raise my eyes to the square spyhole without meeting his, always open and staring.

Still, I suppose there is some fresh air and daylight in this stone box.

11

A s it is not yet daylight, what shall I do with the night? I had an idea. I got up and shone my lamp round the four walls of the cell. They are covered in writing, drawings, peculiar figures, names jumbled together and obscuring each other. It seems every condemned man wanted to leave his mark, here at least. They are in pencil, charcoal, black letters, white, grey, often cut deep into the stone, rust-coloured letters here and there which look as if they are written in blood. If my mind was less preoccupied I would probably be interested in this strange book that unfolds page by page before my eyes across every stone of my dungeon. I would like to piece these fragments of thought scattered across the flagstone together, make them a whole; find the man behind every name; give life and meaning to these mutilated inscriptions, dismembered phrases, truncated words, these bodies without heads like those who wrote them.

Beside where I sleep are two loving hearts pierced with an arrow, and written above them: "Love of my life." The poor soul's relationship didn't last very long.

Next to it a sort of tricorne hat with a little figure drawn crudely beneath, and the words: "Long live the Emperor! 1824."*

More loving hearts, with this inscription, typical in a prison: "I love and worship Mathieu Danvin. JACQUES."

On the wall opposite you can see this name: "Papavoine".* The capital *P* is carefully decorated with fancy arabesques.

A verse from an obscene song.

A liberty bonnet carved quite deeply in the stone, with this underneath: *Bories – La République.* It was one of the four non-commissioned officers from La Rochelle. Poor young man! How repulsive their so-called political necessities are! For the sake of an idea, a daydream, an abstract theory, this terrible reality called the guillotine! And here I am complaining, a wretch who committed a real crime, who shed blood!

I'm not going to look at any more. Scribbled in white in one corner I have just seen an appalling image, a picture of the scaffold which at this very moment is perhaps being set up for me. I almost dropped the lamp.

12

I SAT DOWN HURRIEDLY on the straw again, head on my knees. Then my childish terror disappeared, and I was seized with a strange curiosity to carry on reading the walls.

From beside Papavoine's name I dragged away an enormous spider's web, thick with dust and hanging from a corner. Beneath the web were four or five names, perfectly legible among others which were now just smears on the wall: "DAUTUN, 1815. POULAIN, 1818. JEAN MARTIN, 1821. CASTAING, 1823." As I read these names bleak memories came back to me: Dautun, who cut his brother to pieces and went round Paris at night, throwing the head in a fountain and the torso in a sewer; Poulain, who murdered his wife; Jean Martin, who shot his father with a pistol as the old man was opening the window; Castaing, the doctor who poisoned a friend of his and, while looking after him during his final illness which he himself had caused, gave him more poison instead of medicine; and next to them, Papavoine, the dreadful lunatic who killed children by stabbing them in the head with a knife!

So, I thought – and a clammy shudder ran down my spine – these are the ones who occupied the cell before me. It's here, on the same stone floor where I am now, that they thought their last thoughts, those bloody murderers! It's round these four cramped walls that their last steps were taken, like a wild animal's. They followed each other at short intervals; it seems this dungeon is always full. They kept it warm, and it was for me they did so. Soon it will be my turn to join them in the cemetery at Clamart where the grass grows so tall!

I'm not a visionary, or superstitious. It's probably my thoughts that made me feverish, but as I was dreaming in this way it suddenly seemed as if all those fateful names were written on the black wall in fire; a ringing noise broke out in my ears, getting faster and faster; a reddish glow shone in my eyes; and then it was as if the dungeon was full of men, strange men holding their heads in their left hands, holding it by the mouth because there was no hair. They all shook their fist at me, except the parricide.*

I closed my eyes in horror, and then I saw everything more clearly.

Dream, vision or reality, I would have gone mad if a sudden sensation hadn't woken me in time. I was about to fall over backwards when I felt a cold belly and small hairy feet crawling across my bare foot: it was the spider I had disturbed, running away.

It brought me back to my senses – O, those terrible ghosts! – No, it was a chimera, the imaginings of my empty, fitful mind. An illusion of the Macbeth variety. The dead are dead, especially those. They are well and truly shut up in their mausoleum. It isn't the sort of prison you can escape from. So why should I be so frightened?

The door of the tomb doesn't open from the inside.

13

I N THE LAST FEW DAYS I saw something dreadful.

It was barely daybreak and the prison was full of noise. You could hear heavy doors opening and shutting, iron bolts and padlocks grating, keys jangling on jailers' belts, staircases shaking from top to bottom with hurrying footsteps, voices calling and answering from both ends of the long corridors. My neighbours in the other dungeons, the convicts in irons, were more cheerful than usual. All Bicêtre seemed to be laughing, singing, running, dancing.

The only silent one among the uproar, the only one not part of the commotion, I listened closely, amazed.

A jailer came past.

I took the risk of calling out to him, asked if there was a celebration in the prison.

"Call it a celebration if you like," he answered. "Today's when they put the irons on the convicts who are leaving for Toulon tomorrow. Come see if you want, it'll distract you."

For a solitary such a sight was actually a piece of luck, repellent though it may have been. I took up his offer of entertainment.

The jailer went through the usual procedures to secure me, then led me to a small, totally empty cell that had a barred window, but a proper one at chest height from which you could see real sky.

"There you are," he said. "In here you can see and hear. You've got a box to yourself like the King."

Then he went out and locked, bolted and padlocked me in.

The window looked onto a fairly large square courtyard, surrounded on all four sides by a tall six-storey stone building, like by a wall. No more sordid, more naked, more miserable a sight than these four façades with a vast number of barred windows in them, against which were pressed, from top to bottom, a host of thin pallid faces jammed against each other like stones in a wall, and as it were framed by the criss-crossed iron bars. It was the prisoners, the audience for this ceremony while waiting their turn to play a part. You would have thought they were lost souls, looking out at hell from the little windows of purgatory.

In silence they watched the empty courtyard. They were waiting. Here and there among the drained, despondent faces were a few piercing gazes, as vivid as the tip of a flame.

The square of prisons that surrounds the courtyard does not form a solid wall. One of the four sides (the one that faces east) is divided in the middle, and connecting the two halves is just an iron grille. This grille opens onto a second courtyard, smaller than the first and, like that one, closed off by walls and blackened gables.

All round the main courtyard are stone benches against the wall. In the middle stands a curved metal pole, used to hold a lamp.

Midday struck. The gate of a large carriage entrance hidden beneath a recess suddenly opened. A cart, escorted by some species of filthy, contemptible soldiers in blue uniforms, red epaulettes and yellow cross-straps, rumbled into the courtyard with a loud clanking noise. It was the galley chains and fetters.

At that moment, as if the noise had reawoken all the noise of the prison, the onlookers at the windows, up until now silent and still, burst into shouts of joy, into song, threats and curses mixed with roars of laughter that were heartbreaking to hear. From their expressions you would have thought you were seeing devils. Every face was scowling, every fist came through the bars, every voice yelled, every eye blazed, I was horrified to see so many sparks reappearing among these ashes.

Meanwhile the coppers – among whom you could make out, from their clean clothes and look of horror, a few inquisitive people from Paris – quietly got on with their work. One of them climbed onto the cart and threw down the chains and collars for the journey and bundles of canvas trousers to the others. Then they divided up the work among themselves: some went to a corner of the yard and laid out the long chains which in their jargon they called *strings*, others spread out the taffeta on the cobbles, the shirts and trousers, while, under the eye of the captain, a short stocky old man, the most experienced ones examined the iron collars and shackles one by one and then tested them, making them glint on the cobblestones. All to the mocking cheers of the prisoners, whose voices were drowned out only by the laughter of the convicts for whom all this was being prepared, and who could be seen at the windows of the old prison that looked onto the small courtyard where they had been put.

When the preparations were finished a gentleman in silver braid, whom they called *Monsieur l'Inspecteur*, gave an order to the prison governor, and the next moment, almost simultaneously, two or three low doors belched forth hordes of hideous, howling, ragged men into the courtyard like blasts of hot air. They were the convicts.

At their appearance, yet more delight at the windows. A few of them, the big names of the penal colony, were greeted with cheers and applause that they took with a sort of modest pride. Most of them had a kind of hat that they had plaited together using the straw from their dungeons, each a bizarre shape so that in the towns they passed through it would get their face noticed. These attracted even more applause. One in particular aroused a frenzy of enthusiasm: a young man of seventeen with the face of a young girl. He had just left the dungeon where he had been in solitary confinement for a week; from his bale of straw he had made himself a set of clothes that covered him from head to foot, and came into the courtyard turning cartwheels with the agility of a snake. He was a strolling player convicted of theft. There was furious clapping and yells of delight. The convicts returned it; it was a frightening thing, this exchange of high spirits between official and prospective convicts. Well might society have been there in the shape of the jailers and horrified onlookers, but crime thumbed its nose at it, turning this terrible punishment into a family celebration.

As they arrived they were driven one by one between two lines of warders into the small barred courtyard where doctors were waiting to examine them. This was where they made one last effort to get out of the journey, using health as an excuse, bad eyes, a leg injury, a crippled hand. But they were almost always found fit for hard labour, and so they resigned themselves quite cheerfully, forgetting in minutes their so-called lifelong disability.

The grille to the small courtyard opened again. A guard called the roll in alphabetical order; they came out one by one, each convict went and stood in line in a corner of the large courtyard next to a companion selected for him at random by the first letter of his name. In this way each is left to his own devices; each bears his shackles by himself, side by side with a stranger; and if by chance a convict has a friend, the chain separates them. The last word in misery!

When about thirty had come out they closed the grille again. A copper lined them up with his cane, threw a shirt, jacket and trousers in front of each of them, made a gesture and they all started undressing. Then, as if to order, an unexpected event turned their humiliation into torment.

Up till then the weather had been quite good, and if the October breeze made it chilly, now and then it opened up a gap in the misty grey cloud, letting a ray of sunshine through. But barely had the convicts stripped off their prison rags, the moment they exposed their nudity to the mistrustful inspection of the guards, to the curious gaze of the strangers who hovered round to get a look at their shoulders, the sky turned black and a cold autumn shower suddenly began to fall, pouring onto the square courtyard in torrents, onto the bare heads, the naked bodies of the convicts, onto their pitiful smocks laid out on the cobbles.

In a flash the yard emptied of everyone except convicts and coppers. The curious Parisians took shelter in doorways.

Meanwhile the rain came down in buckets. All you could see in the yard was convicts, naked and soaking on the cobblestones. Their noisy bluster gave way to mournful silence. They shivered, their teeth chattered; their scrawny legs, their knobbly knees knocked together; it was pitiful to see them cover themselves with soaking-wet shirts, jackets and trousers that dripped water. It would have been better to be naked.

Only one, an old man, held on to a little cheerfulness. Wiping himself with his wet shirt, he shouted, "That wasn't on the programme!" Then he began to laugh and shook his fist at the sky.

When they had put their travelling clothes on they were led away in groups of twenty or thirty to the far side of the yard where, stretched out on the ground, their chains were waiting. These chains are long and strong, joined from both sides every two feet by two other, shorter chains at the end of which is fixed a square iron collar that opens by means of a hinge at one corner, and closes at the opposite corner with an iron nut and bolt, riveted to the convict's neck for the whole journey. When the chains are unrolled on the ground they look rather like the backbone of an enormous fish.

They made the convicts sit in the mud on the soaking-wet cobbles; they tried the collars on them; then two blacksmiths from the chain gang, equipped with portable anvils, cold-riveted them on with great blows from iron sledgehammers. It was an appalling moment that made even the most fearless blanch. Every blow of the hammer, struck on the anvil resting on their back, made the poor man's chin leap forwards; the slightest backwards movement and his skull would be smashed open like a nutshell.

After this process they became stony-faced. All you could hear was the jingle of chains, occasionally a cry and the dull sound of the warders' canes on the limbs of the uncooperative. Some were crying; the old ones trembled and bit their lips. In horror I stared at all those grim profiles in their iron frames.

So after the doctors' examination came the jailers' examination; after the jailers' examination, the fitting of the irons. It was a show in three acts.

The sun came out again. You would have thought it had set light to their brains. As if in a convulsion the convicts got up all at once. The five galley chains were fastened to their hands, and suddenly formed an enormous ring round the lamp-post. They went round and round till it strained your eyes. They sang a galley song, a ballad in slang, to a tune that was now wistful, now violent and cheerful; periodically you could hear shrill cries, roars of racked, breathless laughter mingled with mysterious words; then wild cheers; the rhythmic clanking of the chains acted as an orchestra for this song more raucous than the noise they made. If I were looking for an image of a witches' sabbath I couldn't have wished for better or worse.

A large tub was brought into the yard. With blows from their canes the warders broke up the convicts' dance and took them over to the tub, in which you could see some kind of herbs swimming around in some kind of filthy, steaming liquid. They ate.

Once they had eaten they threw what was left of the soup and greyish-brown bread on the cobblestones and began to sing and dance again. They are apparently allowed this freedom on the day the shackles are fitted and during that night.

I watched this bizarre performance with such avid, such thrilled, such searching curiosity that I quite forgot myself. A great feeling of pity shook me to the core, their laughter made me weep.

Suddenly, from amid the deep reverie into which I had sunk I saw the howling circle stop and fall silent. All eyes turned to the window where I was standing. "The condemned one! The condemned one!" they shouted, pointing at me, and there was another, louder outburst of delight.

I stood there, petrified.

I don't know where they knew me from or how they recognized me.

"Good morning! Good evening!" they shouted with their dreadful sniggers. One of the youngest, sentenced to hard labour for life, his face aglow and leaden, looked at me enviously and said: "He's lucky! He's about to be trimmed! Goodbye, comrade!"

I can't say what was going on inside me. It was right – I was their comrade. La Grève is Toulon's sister. I was even lower down the scale than them: they were honouring me. I shuddered.

Yes, their comrade! And a few days' later I could have been enter-tainment for them.

I stayed at the window, motionless, numb, paralysed. But when I saw the five chain gangs move forwards, rushing towards me with words of diabolical affection, when I heard the thunderous din of their shackles, their clamouring, their footsteps at the base of the wall, I thought this horde of demons was scrambling its way up to my miserable cell; I gave a scream, flung myself at the door hard enough to break it down – but there was no way out. It was bolted on the outside. I hammered, I cried out furiously. It seemed as if I could hear the terrifying voices of the convicts coming closer. I thought I saw their hideous faces appear over the window sill, I gave another cry of horror and passed out.

14

WHEN I CAME ROUND it was dark. I was lying on a pallet; in the light of a lamp swaying on the ceiling I saw rows of other pallets either side of mine. I realized I had been taken to the infirmary.

For a moment or two I lay awake, although without thinking or remembering anything. At any other time this prison hospital bed would have doubtless made me shrink back in disgust and pity, but I was no longer the man I used to be. The sheets were grey and rough, the blanket thin and full of holes; you could smell straw through the mattress – but so what! Between these coarse sheets my limbs could relax; beneath this blanket, thin though it was, I could feel the dreadful cold in my very bones that I had grown used to gradually wearing off. Then I fell asleep again.

I was woken by a loud noise; it was daybreak. The noise was coming from outside; my bed was by the window, I sat up to see what it was.

The window looked out onto the great courtyard of Bicêtre. The courtyard was full of people; in the middle of the crowd two lines of veteran troops were struggling to keep a narrow pathway clear across the yard. Between the double ranks of soldiers, five long carts full of men slowly made their way, jolted by every cobblestone. It was the convicts leaving.

None of the carts had a roof. Each was occupied by one chain gang. The convicts sat on either edge facing outwards, back to back, separated by the communal chain which was laid out down the middle of the wagon, and on each end of which, foot resting on it, stood a copper with a loaded rifle. You could hear the irons clink, and every time the carriage shook you saw their heads and their dangling legs bob and bounce about.

A fine, penetrating rain chilled the air, making their grey, now black canvas trousers cling to their knees. Water streamed from their long beards, their short hair; their faces were purple; you could see them shivering, teeth grinding with rage and cold. It wasn't possible to move anything else. Once riveted to the chain you were just one tiny part of the monstrous whole known as the line, which moved as a single man. The mind was forced into submission, the iron collar of the penal colony condemned it to death; as for the creature itself, from now on its needs and appetites could only be at set times. And so, motionless, for the most part half-naked, bareheaded, legs dangling, they began their twenty-five day journey on the same carts, wearing the same clothes in the blazing July heat as in the cold November rain. You would have thought that man wanted the heavens to do half the executioner's work for him.

Between the crowd and the carts a kind of awful dialogue had sprung up: abuse from one side, bravado from the other, curses from both; but at a sign from the captain I saw canes rain down at random on the carts, on shoulders or heads, and everything went back to that state of superficial calm known as order. But the eyes were full of revenge, the wretched men's fists clenched on their knees.

Escorted by mounted police and ordinary bobbies on foot, one by one the five carts disappeared under the tall arched gateway of Bicêtre; a sixth followed, in which large cooking pots, copper mess tins and spare chains and shackles bounced about, all jumbled together. A few warders who had lingered on in the canteen came rushing out to rejoin their squad. The crowd dispersed. The whole spectacle vanished like a figment of the imagination. You could hear the heavy sound of the wheels and the horses' hooves on the cobbled road from Fontainebleau getting progressively fainter, along with the crack of the whips, the clank of the chains and the yells of people wishing the convicts bad luck for their journey.

And for them this was just the start!

What was it that lawyer said to me? Hard labour! Ah, yes! Better death, a thousand times! Better the scaffold than the penal colony, better oblivion than hell; better to offer up my neck to Guillotin's blade than to the chain gang's iron yoke! Hard labour? Good God!

15

SADLY I WASN'T ILL. I had to leave the infirmary. The dungeon reclaimed me.

Not ill! No, I was young, healthy and strong. The blood coursed freely in my veins; my limbs obeyed my every whim; I was sound in mind and body; made for a long life – yes, all this is true, and yet I had a disease, a fatal disease, a disease created by man.

Since leaving the infirmary I've had a harrowing thought, a thought that is enough to drive me mad – that if they had left me there I might have been able to escape. The doctors, the good sisters seemed interested in me. To die so young, and from such a death! You would have thought they felt sorry for me, the way they fussed round my bed all the time. Bah! Curiosity! Besides, people who cure, they can cure you of fever but not of a death sentence. Yet it would have been so easy for them! A door left open! What harm would it have done them?

No chance now! My appeal will be rejected, because everything is in order: the witnesses did their witnessing, the pleaders their pleading, the judges their judging. I'm of no importance, unless… No, that's madness! No hope now! An appeal is a rope on which you dangle above the abyss; every second you hear it fraying until it snaps. It's as if the blade of the guillotine took six weeks to fall.

But what if I got my pardon? To get my pardon! But who from? And why? And how? It would be impossible for them to pardon me. As they say, it's an example!

I have only three steps to take now: Bicêtre, the Conciergerie, La Grève.

16

D URING THE FEW HOURS I spent in the infirmary I sat by the window in the sun – it had come out again – or at least as much sun as the bars on the windows let me have.

There I was, holding a head that was heavy and full of turmoil in hands that were already too full, elbows on my knees, feet on the crossbars of the chair, because despondency made me bend double, curl up as if I no longer had bones in my limbs or muscles in my flesh.

The stifling prison smell choked me more than ever; I could still hear the noise of the convicts' chains; I felt the great weariness of Bicêtre. I thought the Good Lord ought to take pity on me and at least send a little bird to sing to me on the roof across the way.

I don't know whether it was the Good Lord or the Devil who answered my prayers, but at almost that same moment I heard a voice beneath my window, not a bird, much better than that: the pure, clear, velvety voice of a girl of fifteen. I looked up with a start, listened eagerly to her song. It was a slow, sleepy tune, a kind of sorrowful and tragic crooning; these are the words:

"As I was strolling down the lane
Three blighters collared me,
Tirra-woe-lirra-lee.
Dirty coppers, they're all the same,
Tirra-woe-lirra-lay.
Banged me up an' lost the key,
Tirra-woe-lirra-lee."

I can't describe how bitterly disappointed I felt. The voice went on:

"Banged me up an' lost the key,
Tirra-woe-lirra-lee,
Ropes around me wrists an' all,
Tirra-woe-lirra-lay.
All of Bow Street had a ball,
Tirra-woe-lirra-lee.
Then I clocks this boat race, we was pally,
Tirra-woe-lirra-lay,
Some old tea leaf from down our alley,
Tirra-woe-lirra-lee.

"Says I to this tea leaf, oi matey,
Tirra-woe-lirra-lee,
Go tell me old trouble an' strife,
Tirra-woe-lirra-lay,
I'm in the bucket, this time it's for life,
Tirra-woe-lirra-lee.
My old woman, she went off 'er 'ead,
Tirra-woe-lirra-lay,
What you gorn an' done this time? she said,
Tirra-woe-lirra-lee.

"What you gorn an' done this time? says she,
Tirra-woe-lirra-lee.
I done for a bloke, they nabbed me red-'anded,
Tirra-woe-lirra-lay,
'Alf-inched 'is bees, fine an' dandy,
Tirra-woe-lirra-lee,
'Is bees an' 'is gordon, it's 'andsome,
Tirra-woe-lirra-lay,
An' silver buckles, worth a king's ransom,
Tirra-woe-lirra-lee.

"Nice fancy buckles, my eye,
Tirra-woe-lirra-lee.
But 'er indoors she runs off down Versailles,
Tirra-woe-lirra-lay,
Gets it into 'er 'ead to earwig the King,
Tirra-woe-lirra-lee,
Tells him some porkies, says she'll do anything,
Tirra-woe-lirra-lay,
To get me out the dog's dinner I'm in,
Tirra-woe-lirra-lee.

"Out this dog's dinner, too right,
Tirra-woe-lirra-lee,
An' if my old lady can swing it, that night,
Tirra-woe-lirra-lay,
I'll take her to church an' we'll be man an' wife,
Tirra-woe-lirra-lee.
Give 'er ribbons an' lace, me old trouble an' strife,
Tirra-woe-lirra-lay,
An' diamond slippers for 'er dainty feet,
Tirra-woe-lirra-lee.

"Diamond slippers for my better 'alf,
Tirra-woe-lirra-lee.
But 'is 'ighness the Gaffer, he didn't laugh,
Tirra-woe-lirra-lay,
By my best titfer, he says, for your cheek,

26

Tirra-woe-lirra-lee,
Your pot an' pan's for it by the end of the week,
Tirra-woe-lirra-lay,
I'll make him dance on air, you'll see.
Tirra-woe-lirra-lee."

I didn't listen; I couldn't have listened to another word. That dreadful lament with its partly intelligible, partly hidden meaning, the ruffian's struggle with the police patrol, the thief he meets and then sends off to his wife with the appalling message: "I killed a man and I've been arrested" – "I done for a bloke, they nabbed me red-'anded"; the wife who rushes off to Versailles with a petition and the King who gets annoyed and threatens to make the guilty man "dance on air"; and all to the sweetest tune by the sweetest voice that ever beguiled a human ear!... I sat there distraught, blood turned to ice, overwhelmed. It was revolting, such vile words coming from that sweet ruby-red mouth. It was like a slug's trail on a rose.

I can't express what I felt; I was distressed and soothed all at once. The jargon of the cave, the penal colony, that grotesque and bloody slang coupled with the voice of a young girl, a graceful transition from the voice of a child to the voice of a woman! All those deformed, misshapen words, so tuneful, rhythmical, exquisite!

Oh, how unspeakable prison is! It has a poison in it that defiles everything. Everything gets blackened, even a fifteen-year-old girl's song! You find a bird, it has muck on its wings; you pick a pretty flower, you smell it: it stinks.

17

OH! IF I ESCAPED, how I would run through the fields! No, you mustn't run. It would make people stare, make them suspicious. On the contrary, walk slowly, hold your head up, sing. Make sure to wear an old blue smock with red patterns on. It's a good disguise. All the market gardeners hereabouts wear them.

Not far from Arcueil I know a clump of trees by a marsh, where my friends from school and I used to go and catch frogs every Thursday. That is where I would hide till evening.

Once it got dark I would set off again. I would go to Vincennes. No, the river is in the way. I would go to Arpajon – it would be better to head for Saint-Germain, go to Le Havre and catch a boat to England – but so what? I get to Longjumeau, a policeman comes by, he asks for my passport... I'm done for!

Ah! Miserable dreamer, first knock down the three-foot-thick wall that imprisons you! Death! Death!

And to think that as a boy I came here to Bicêtre to see the great well and all the lunatics!

18

WHILE I WAS WRITING ALL THIS,* my lamp grew dim, it got light, the chapel clock struck six.

What does it mean? The duty jailer just came into my dungeon, took off his cap, said good morning, apologized for disturbing me and asked, doing his best to soften his harsh voice, what I would like for breakfast?...

A sudden shiver ran through me: will it be today?

19

IT'S TODAY!

The prison governor paid me a personal visit. He asked if there was any way in which he could be kind or helpful to me, said he hoped I had no complaints about him or his staff, enquired in some detail about my health, whether I had slept well; then as he was going he called me "Monsieur"!

It's today!

20

THAT JAILER DOESN'T THINK I have any reason to complain about him or his assistant jailers. He is right. It would be wrong to complain; they have done their job, they have looked after me properly; after all, they were polite when I arrived and when I left. Why would I not be satisfied?

That good jailer with his kindly smile, soothing words, those eyes that fawn and spy on you, with his big podgy hands, he is prison personified, Bicêtre incarnate. Everything around me is a prison; I see prison in all its forms, human as well as in the shape of bolts and bars. This wall is a prison made of stone; this door, a prison of wood; these jailers, a prison of flesh and blood. Prison is a sort of terrible creature, whole, inseparable, half house half man. I am its prey: it broods over me, clutches me to its innermost recesses. It shuts me inside its granite walls, locks me in with its iron locks, watches over me with its jailer's eyes.

Oh, wretch! What will become of me? What are they going to do to me?

21

I AM CALM NOW. It's all over and done with. I have come through the terrible state of anxiety that the governor's visit plunged me into. Because I admit I was still hoping – but now, thank God, I have no more hope.

This is what just happened:

As it was striking half-past six – no, it was quarter to – the door of my dungeon opened again. A white-haired old man wearing a brown frock coat came in. The coat was half open. I saw bands, a cassock. It was a priest.

This priest wasn't the prison chaplain. It was ominous.

He sat down facing me with a kindly smile; then shook his head and raised his eyes to heaven, in other words the vaulted ceiling of the dungeon. I understood.

"Are you prepared, my son?" he said.

I answered in a weak voice:

"I'm not prepared, but I'm ready."

Meanwhile my eyes blurred over, I broke out in a cold sweat all over, I could feel my forehead about to burst, my ears buzzing.

As I swayed to and fro on my chair as if dropping off to sleep, the kind old man talked. At least that's how it seemed; I think I remember his lips moving, his hands fidgeting, his eyes shining.

The door opened a second time. The noise of the bolts dragged me from my daze, him from his words. A gentleman in a black tailcoat appeared, accompanied by the prison governor, and bowed deeply to me. The man's face had something of the official sadness of an undertaker. In his hand was a roll of paper.

"Monsieur," he said, smiling politely, "I am an usher to the Royal Court of Paris. I have the honour to bring you a message from His Worship the Public Prosecutor."

The initial shock was over. I regained my presence of mind.

"Is it His Worship the Public Prosecutor," I replied, "who is so determined to have my head? All the more honour for me that he should write to me. I hope my death will please him greatly. Because I would hate to think that he had sought it with such zeal if it was a matter of indifference to him."

I said all this and then added firmly:

"Read, Monsieur!"

He began reading out a long text, his voice lilting at the end of each sentence and hesitating over every word. It was the rejection of my appeal.

"The sentence will be carried out today on the Place de Grève," he added when he had finished, without looking up from the stamped and sealed piece of paper. "We will leave for the Conciergerie at exactly half-past seven. Will you be so kind as to come with me, my dear Monsieur?"

For a moment or two I hadn't been listening. The governor was talking to the priest; his eyes were fixed on the piece of paper; I looked at the door, which was still half open... Ah, wretched me! Four riflemen in the corridor!

The usher repeated his question, this time looking at me.

"As you wish," I replied. "Whenever you like!"

He bowed and said:

"It will be my honour to come for you in half an hour."

Then they left me on my own.

My God, a way out! Any way! I've got to escape! I have to! Right away! Out of the door, out the window, out the roof! Even though I would leave parts of myself on the beams on the way!

A plague on it! Hell and damnation! It would take months to make a hole in the wall using proper tools – and I don't have a nail, let alone an hour!

22

H ERE I AM, *transferred,* as the report puts it.
But the journey is worth describing.

Half-past seven was striking when the usher reappeared in the doorway of my dungeon. "I await you, Monsieur," he said. Him and others, unfortunately!

I stood up, took a step; I thought I wouldn't be able to take another, my head was so heavy, my legs so weak. But I pulled myself together and walked quite steadily. Before leaving the dungeon I glanced round one last time – I loved my dungeon – then I left it open and empty; which makes a dungeon look rather odd.

But it won't stay that way for long. They are expecting someone this evening, so the turnkeys were saying, a condemned man who the Crown Court are in the process of dealing with at this very moment.

The chaplain joined us along the corridor. He had been having breakfast.

As we came out of the jail the governor took me affectionately by the hand, and then added four veteran soldiers to my escort.

At the door to the infirmary an old man who was dying called out to me: "Till we meet again!"

We reached the courtyard. I took a deep breath; it did me good.

We didn't have far to go in the fresh air. A carriage drawn by post horses was standing in the first courtyard; the same carriage that brought me here, a kind of long cabriolet divided crossways into two compartments by a wire grille so thick you would think it had been knitted. Both sections have a door, one at the front of the carriage, the other at the rear. The whole thing so filthy, so black, so full of dust that the paupers' hearse is a coronation coach by comparison.

Before burying myself in this tomb on two wheels I gave a quick look round the courtyard, one of those desperate looks that threaten to make walls come crashing down. The courtyard, a kind of small square planted with trees, was already packed with an audience as big as for the convicts. A crowd already!

Like on the day the chain gang left an autumn rain was falling, that same fine, icy rain which is falling as I write, which will probably keep falling all day, which will carry on for longer than me.

The roads were awash, the courtyard a quagmire. I enjoyed seeing the crowds in all the mud.

The usher and a policeman climbed into the front compartment; the priest, myself and another policeman into the other. Four mounted police round the carriage. Not counting the driver, it was eight men for one man.

As I was getting in, a grey-eyed old woman said: "I like this better than the chain gang."

I understand her. This is a sight that you can take in at a glance more easily, it's seen in a moment. It's much nicer, more convenient. There is nothing to distract you. There is just one man, and heaped on that single man as much misery as on all the penal convicts put together. Only this is less diluted – a strong liqueur, much more appetizing.

The carriage set off. It made a muffled noise as it went under the archway of the great gate then came out into the street, and the heavy doors of Bicêtre closed behind it. I was overcome by torpor, like a man in a state of inertia who can't move or call out as he hears himself being buried. I vaguely heard the clusters of little bells round the necks of the post horses jingling rhythmically in snatches, the steel-rimmed wheels mumbling on the cobbles or thumping against the body of the carriage as it went in and out of ruts, the melodious gallop of the police horses round the coach, the crack of the coachman's whip. It felt like a whirlwind carrying me away.

Through the wire mesh of a peephole opposite I stared mechanically at the inscription carved in big letters over the great gateway of Bicêtre: "HOME FOR THE AGED". Goodness me, I thought. They have people in there who get old.

And, like you do between waking and sleeping, I turned this thought over and over in my mind, a mind numb with pain. Then as the coach turned off the avenue and onto the main road, the view from the small hatch suddenly changed. The towers of Notre-Dame appeared, blue and half-hidden in the Paris mist. Immediately my mental outlook changed as well. I became a machine like the carriage. The thought of Bicêtre gave way to the thought of Notre-Dame: the people up on the tower where the flag is will have a good view, I said to myself stupidly.

I think it was then that the priest began to talk to me again. Patiently I let him have his say. My ears were already full of the noise of the wheels, the galloping of the horses, the coachman's whip. He was just one more.

32

In silence I listened to the torrent of monotonous words that lulled me into drowsiness like the babbling of a spring, passing me by like bent, twisted elms along the highway, when suddenly the sharp staccato voice of the court usher, who was sitting in the front, shook me out of it.

"Well, Father!" he said in an almost cheerful voice. "What news?"

And he turned to the priest.

The chaplain, who was talking to me non-stop and deafened by the carriage, didn't answer.

"Ah-ha!" the usher went on, raising his voice over the noise of the wheels. "Infernal carriage!"

Infernal indeed!

He went on:

"It's probably all this bumping up and down: you can't hear yourself think. So what was it I was going to say? Would you mind reminding me what I was going to say, Father? – Oh yes! Do you know today's big news in Paris?"

I shuddered, as if it was me he was talking about.

"No," said the priest, who had finally heard, "I didn't have time to read the papers this morning. I'll see it this evening. When I'm busy all day like this I get the porter to keep my papers for me and read them when I get back."

"Really!" the usher went on, "It's not possible that you don't know. The news that's all over Paris! This morning's news!"

Then I spoke up: "I think I know what it is!"

The usher stared at me:

"You? Really? Then what have you got to say about it?"

"You're interested?" I said.

"And why not, Monsieur?" replied the usher. "Everyone has political views. I respect you too highly to think you don't have some of your own. As for me, I'm absolutely of the opinion that they should re-establish the *garde nationale*.* I used to be a sergeant in my company, and, well, it was really most enjoyable."

I put in:

"I didn't think that was what it was about."

"So what is it then? You're saying you've heard the news?..."

"I'm talking about something else that Paris is interested in today."

The fool didn't understand, but his curiosity was aroused.

"Other news? Where the blazes do you get news from? What news, for pity's sake my dear Monsieur? Do you know what it is, Father? Are you better informed than me? Do please give me all the facts. What's it about? – I love news, you see. I tell His Worship the judge all about it, it amuses him."

And so much other nonsense. He turned first to the priest then to me, but my response was just to shrug.

"So!" he said to me. "What is it you're thinking of?"

"I'm thinking," I replied, "that tonight I won't be thinking any more."

"Ah, that's what it is!" he retorted. "Come along now, you're too gloomy! Monsieur Castaing chatted."

Then, after a pause:

"I accompanied Monsieur Papavoine. He had his otter-skin cap on and smoked a cigar. As for the boys from La Rochelle, they only talked to each other. But they did talk."

There was another pause then he carried on:

"Madmen! Fanatics! They behaved as if everyone was beneath them. And you, you seem very solemn to me, young man."

"Young man?" I said, "I'm older than you are; every quarter of an hour that goes by makes me a year older."

He turned round, looked at me in gauche amazement for a moment then gave a loud, nervous laugh.

"Come off it, older than me, you must be joking! I could be your grandfather."

"I'm not joking," I replied, seriously.

He opened his snuffbox.

"Here, my dear Monsieur, don't be angry; take a pinch of snuff, don't hold a grudge against me."

"Don't worry; I won't be holding it for long."

Just then his snuffbox, which he was offering me, knocked against the wire grille between us. A sudden jolt sent it flying and it landed upside down with the lid open at the policeman's feet.

"Damned grille!" exclaimed the usher.

He turned to me.

"Really! That's just my luck! I've lost all my snuff!"

"I'm losing more than you," I replied with a smile.

He tried to gather up his snuff, muttering under his breath:

"More than me! That's easy to say. No snuff all the way to Paris! It's terrible!"

The chaplain comforted him for a moment; I don't know if I had other things on my mind but it seemed like a continuation of the exhortation that had first been addressed to me. The priest and the usher gradually got into conversation; I left them to talk and got on with thinking.

As we reached the toll gates I was no doubt still preoccupied, but somehow Paris seemed noisier than usual.

The carriage stopped briefly at the city toll. The customs officers inspected it. If it had been a sheep or a bullock being taken for slaughter we would have had to slip them some cash; but a man's head isn't subject to duty. They waved us through.

After crossing the boulevard the coach plunged at full trot into the winding old streets of the Faubourg Saint-Marceau and La Cité, which twist and turn like the tunnels of an ants' nest. The rumbling of the carriage was so loud and so fast over the cobbles of the narrow streets that I couldn't hear the noise from outside. When I glanced out the small square hatch it seemed the streams of passers-by were stopping to look at the carriage, that gangs of children were chasing after it. Now and then I thought I saw a man or an old woman, sometimes the two together, standing on a crossroads here and there, mouths open wide as if to give a loud shout, and holding a bundle of printed sheets* that passers-by were fighting over.

Half-past eight was just striking on the clock at the Palais de Justice as we arrived in the courtyard of the Conciergerie. The sight of the great staircase, the black chapel, the grim-looking grilles made my blood run cold. When the carriage stopped I thought my heart was going to stop beating too.

I braced myself; I jumped down from my dungeon on wheels and hurried under the archway between two lines of soldiers. There was already a crowd waiting to see me come past.

23

A S I WALKED through the public galleries of the Palais de Justice I almost felt free and easy; but my resolve failed me when low doors, hidden staircases, inner passageways, long, hushed, muffled corridors opened up in front of me, places where only those who condemn or who are condemned ever go.

The usher stayed with me. The priest had gone off and would come back in two hours' time; he had business to attend to.

They took me to the chief constable's office, into whose charge the usher delivered me. It was an exchange. The chief constable asked him to wait a moment, saying he was going to have some *game* to hand over to him so he could take it straight to Bicêtre in the same carriage on its way back. Probably today's condemned prisoner, the one who would spend tonight on the bale of straw that I hadn't had time to wear out.

"Very well," the usher said to the chief constable, "I'll wait for a while; we can do both reports at once, that works out nicely."

Meanwhile I was put in a small office next to the chief constable's. They left me alone, safely under lock and key.

I don't know where my thoughts were or how long I had been in there when a sudden wild roar of laughter in my ear woke me from my dreams.

I looked up with a shudder. I wasn't alone in the cell any more. There was another man with me, a man of about fifty-five, medium height, wrinkled, stooping, going grey; thickset, with a shifty look in his grey eyes, a bitter smile on his face; filthy dirty, in rags, half-naked, revolting to look at.

It seemed the door had opened, spewed him out, and then closed again without my noticing. If only death could come like that!

The man and I stared at each other for a moment – him still laughing that laugh of his, which sounded like a death rattle; me half astonished, half afraid.

"Who are you?" I said, eventually.

"Funny question!" he replied. "A *friauche*."*

"A *friauche*! What does that mean?"

My question made him even more cheerful than before.

"It means," he exclaimed, roaring with laughter, "that the stretch is going to play baskets with my sorbonne in six weeks time, the same as he's going to do with your crust in six hours – ha ha! Looks like you understand now."

It was true, I had gone white, my hair stood on end. He was the other condemned man, today's condemned man, the one they were waiting for at Bicêtre, my successor.

"What can I say? Here's my story. I'm the son of an honest tea leaf; it's a pity Charlot* went to the trouble of tying his cravat on him one day. That was in the reign of the gibbet, by the grace of God. By the time I was six I didn't have a mother or father; in summer I used to turn cartwheels in the dust by the roadside so people might throw me a sou from the door of the post-chaise; in winter I went barefoot in the mud, blowing on my fingers that were red with cold; you could see my thighs through my trousers. When I was nine I started making use of my shifties,* I emptied a digger* now and then, I made off with a bit of peel;* by the time I was ten I was a wide boy.* Then I wised up; at seventeen I was a babbling brook.* I bust open a boutie, I bent a turn.* I got nabbed. I was old enough, they sent me to row in the land navy. It's hard, the chain gang; sleeping on a board, living on black bread and water, dragging a stupid ball and chain around for no reason; sticks and sun beating down on you. And on top of that they shave your head, and me with my lovely chestnut-brown hair! Never mind!... I did my time. Fifteen years, it takes it out of you. I was thirty-two. One fine morning they gave me a ticket and the sixty-six francs I'd managed to earn myself from fifteen years' hard labour, working sixteen hours a day, thirty days a month, twelve months a year. Be that as it may, I wanted to go straight with my sixty-six francs, I had finer feelings under my rags and tatters than you'll find under a crow's floorcloth.* But they'd put the mockers on my passport! It was yellow, and they'd written *discharged convict* in it. I had to produce it everywhere I went, and show it every week to the mayor of the village where they made me crouch.* A nice reference that was! An ex-con! I frightened folk, little children ran away from me, everyone shut their doors. No one wanted to give me work. I ate my sixty-six francs. And then I had to live. I showed them my two good strong arms, they slammed the door in my face. I offered to work for fifteen sous a day, for ten sous, five. Nothing. What could I do? One day I was famished. I bunged my elbow through a baker's window; I grabbed a loaf, the baker grabbed me. I never ate the bread and got hard labour for life with three letters branded into my shoulder – I'll show you if you like – they call that sort of justice reoffending. So there I was, an old lag.* They put me back in Toulon, this time with the green caps.* I had to escape. To do it I just had three walls to break through, two chains to cut, and I'd got a nail. I escaped. They let off the alarm cannon;

because us, we're like the cardinals in Rome, dressed in red and they fire a cannon when we leave. Their grapeshot only hit the birds. No yellow passport this time, but no sixty-six francs neither. I met some muckers who'd done their time as well, or snapped their ropes. The pitch and toss* offered to let me join them, they did a lot of relieving on the frog.* I agreed, and started killing for a living. Sometimes it was a stagecoach, sometimes a post-chaise, sometimes a cattle dealer on a horse. We took the money, left the animal or the carriage to take its chance and buried the man under a tree making sure his feet didn't stick out – and then we danced on the grave so the soil didn't look freshly turned over. That's what made me old, living in the undergrowth, sleeping in the open, hunted from wood to wood, but at least I was free, my own man. Everything comes to an end, that just the same as anything else. One fine night the snare merchants* collared us. My chinas cleared off, but me, the oldest, I was left in the claws of the cats with braid on their hats. They brought me here. I've been on every rung of the ladder so far except one. Whether I stole a handkerchief or killed a man, it was all much of a muchness to me from then on in; there was still one punishment for to give me for reoffending. I just had to go see the reaper.* Mine's been a short run. Well, I was getting old and good for nothing no more. My father married the widow,* me, I'm going to retire to the Abbey of Mount-Sorrow.* So there it is, mucker."

I stood there listening, baffled. He began laughing again, even louder than the first time, and went to shake my hand. I drew back in horror.

"Friend," he said, "you don't look none too brave. Don't come the chicken in front of the bulldog.* Oh yes, you'll have a nasty moment on the shelf, but it's soon over and done with. I'd like to be there to show you a trick or two. By all the gods! If they want to reap me with you today I've got a mind not to appeal. The same priest can take care of the both of us; I don't mind having your leftovers. You can see I'm a good lad. Eh! What do you say then? Friends!"

He came towards me again.

"No thank you, Monsieur," I replied, pushing him away.

Yet more laughter at my reply.

"Oh ho! 'Monsieur'. One is a marquis. He's a marquis!"

I stopped him:

"My friend, I need time to myself to think, leave me alone."

My seriousness made him thoughtful all of a sudden. He shook his grey, nearly bald head; then, scratching his hairy chest which could be seen under his open shirt:

"I understand," he mumbled under his breath, "you've got a point, the boar!..."*

Then, after a few minutes silence:

"Look," he said, almost shyly, "you're a marquis, that's fine and dandy; but you've got a handsome frock coat there that ain't going to be much use to you no more! The stretch will take it. Give it me, I can sell it to get some tobacco."

I took off my frock coat and gave it to him. He clapped his hands in childish delight. Then, seeing I was in shirtsleeves and shivering:

"You're cold, Monsieur, put this on; it's raining, you'll get wet – 'sides, you have to look proper on the tumbril."

With that he took off his thick grey woollen jacket and slipped my arms into it for me. I let him do it.

Then I leant against the wall, I couldn't say what effect this man was having on me. He began examining the frock coat I had given him, all the time letting out squeals of delight.

"The pockets are brand new! The collar isn't worn! – I'll get fifteen francs at least – what luck! Tobacco for my whole six weeks!"

The door opened. They had come for both of us: me, to take me to the room where condemned men await their time; him, to go to Bicêtre. Laughing, he stood between the guards who were taking him away and said to the policemen:

"Now don't get it wrong, see: we've changed peel, Monsieur and me – so don't go taking me instead of him. Hell's teeth! That wouldn't suit me at all, not now I've got something to get myself some tobacco with!"

24

THE OLD VILLAIN, he took my frock coat from me – because I didn't give it to him – and left me with this bit of rag, his disgusting jacket. What on earth will I look like?

I didn't let him have my frock coat out of indifference, or charity. No: it was because he was stronger than me. If I had refused he would have hit me with those great big fists of his.

Oh yes of course, charity! I was full of ill feeling. I would have liked to strangle him with my bare hands, the old crook! To crush him under my feet!

My heart is full of anger and bitterness, I can feel it. I think my gall bladder has burst. Death makes us malicious.

25

THEY HAVE PUT ME IN A CELL that has just four walls and, it goes without saying, plenty of bars on the windows and bolts on the door.

I asked for a table and chair, something to write with. They brought me all that.

Then I asked for a bed. The jailer gave me a surprised look as if to say: "What's the point?"

Nonetheless they set up a trestle bed in the corner. But at the same time a policeman came and sat with me in what they called *my room*. Were they afraid I would strangle myself with the mattress?

26

IT IS TEN O'CLOCK.

Oh, my poor little girl! Another six hours and I will be dead! I will be just some hideous thing lying on a slab in a medical school lecture room; a head for someone to take a cast from, a torso for someone else to dissect; then what is left will be crammed into a coffin and the whole lot will be sent off to Clamart.

That is what they are going to do to your father, all these men who don't hate me, who feel sorry for me and could save me. They are going to kill me. Do you realize that, Marie? Kill me in cold blood, with ceremony, for the good of it! Oh, good God!

Poor little thing! Your father who loved you so much, your father who used to kiss your white, sweet-smelling little neck, who was always stroking your curly hair as if it were silk, who would take your pretty round face in his hand, who would dandle you on his knee and put your little hands together every night to pray to God!

Who will do all that for you now? Who will love you? Every child your age has a father except you. On New Year's Day, my child, how will you get used to not having presents, lovely toys, sweets and kisses? How will you get used to not eating and drinking, you unhappy orphan?

Oh! If that jury had at least seen her, my pretty little Marie! They would have realized that you shouldn't kill the father of a three-year-old child.

And when she grows up, if she gets that far, what will become of her? Her father will be just one of the memories that the people of Paris have. She will be ashamed of me and my name; she will be looked down on, rejected, despised on account of me, me who loves her with all my heart. Oh, my beloved little Marie! Is it really true that you will be ashamed of me, loathe me?

Wretch! What a crime I committed, and what a crime I am making society commit!

Oh! Is it really true that I'll be dead before the day is out? Is it really true that it's me? The muffled sound of shouting that I can hear outside, the streams of happy people hurrying along the embankments already, the policemen getting ready in their barracks, the priest in his black robes, that other man with blood on his hands, all that is for me! It is me who is going to die! Me, the very same one who is here, alive, moving, breathing, who is sitting at this table that looks like any other table and could easily be somewhere else; me, in a word, this me who I can touch, who I can feel, who is wearing these creased clothes!

27

IF I AT LEAST KNEW HOW THEY DO IT, how you die there! But the terrible thing is that I don't know.

The name of the thing is appalling, I don't know how I ever managed to write it down or even say it before now.

The combination of those ten letters, what they look like, their appearance, is specially designed to stir up terrible thoughts, and the name of the accursed doctor who invented the thing had something prophetic about it.

The image I associate with this monstrous word is vague, ill defined and all the more sinister as a result. Each syllable is like part of the machinery. In my mind I constantly build and dismantle that hideous structure.

I daren't ask about it, but it's appalling not to know what it is or how to approach it. Apparently there is a bascule and they lay you on your stomach... Oh! My hair will go white even before my head comes off!

28

I DID GET A GLIMPSE OF IT ONCE HOWEVER.
I was driving through the Place de Grève in a carriage one day, around eleven in the morning. All of a sudden the carriage stopped.

There were a lot of people in the square. I stuck my head out the door. A mob thronged La Grève and the embankment – men, women and children were standing on the parapet. Above their heads you could see a sort of platform made of red-coloured wood that three men were building.

A condemned man must have been due to be executed that day, and they were assembling the machinery.

I turned my head away before seeing it. Next to the carriage a woman was saying to a child:

"There, look! The blade isn't running properly, they're going to grease the runners with a piece of candle."

That is probably how far they have got today. It has just struck eleven. No doubt they are greasing the runners.

Ah! This time, wretch, I won't be turning my head away.

29

OH, MY PARDON! My pardon! Maybe they will pardon me. The King has nothing against me. If only they would go and find my lawyer. My lawyer, quickly! I definitely want hard labour. Five years' hard labour and we'll say no more – or twenty years – or life, with the branding iron. But spare my life!

A convict on hard labour can still walk about, come and go, see the sun shine.

30

THE PRIEST CAME BACK.

He has white hair, looks very gentle, a kind and decent face; in fact he is a fine and charitable man. This morning I saw him give everything he had in his purse to the prisoners. Yet how come there is nothing in his voice that stirs you, nothing that is itself stirred? How come he has never said anything that captured my mind or my heart?

This morning I was distraught. I hardly heard a thing he said. His words seemed pointless, they left me indifferent, ran off me like the cold rain on the icy window pane.

Yet when he came back just now it did me good to see him. Among all these men he is the only one who for me is still a man. I was seized with an intense thirst for kind, comforting words.

We sat down, him on the chair, me on the bed. He said: "My son…" – and that one word opened my heart. He went on:

"Do you believe in God, my son?"

"Yes, Father," I replied.

"Do you believe in the Holy, Apostolic, Roman Catholic Church?"

"I'd be glad to," I said.

"You seem to have doubts, my son," he continued.

And then he began to talk. He talked for a long time; he said a lot of words; then when he thought he had finished he stood up and looked at me for the first time since he began speaking, and asked:

"Well?"

I can assure you I had listened to him eagerly at first, then closely, and then devotedly.

I stood up too.

"Leave me alone please, Monsieur," I replied.

He asked:

"When shall I come back?"

"I'll let you know."

And so he went out, not angrily, but just shaking his head as if saying to himself:

"A godless man."

No, as low as I may have sunk I'm not godless, and God is my witness that I believe in him. But what had he said to me, this old man? Nothing sincere, nothing compassionate, nothing to bring tears to

43

your eyes, nothing to rend your soul, nothing that came from his heart into mine, nothing of him to me. Quite the reverse, just something hazy, unspecific, which could be applied to everyone and everything; pompous when what was needed was depth, bland when it should have been simple – a kind of sentimental sermon, a theological dirge. A quote in Roman Latin here and there. St Augustine, St Gregory, how do I know? He seemed to be reciting a text that had been recited many times before, going back over a subject that had been wiped from his memory as a result of being known. No look in his eye, no tone in his voice, no gesture of his hands.

But how could it be otherwise? This priest is the official prison chaplain. Comforting and exhorting is his trade, he earns a living from it. Convicts and sufferers come under the jurisdiction of his eloquence. He hears their confessions and ministers to them because that is his job. He has grown old seeing men to their death. He has long been accustomed to what would make others shudder; his hair, powdered nicely white, doesn't stand on end any more; the galleys and the scaffold are everyday events for him. He is indifferent. He probably has a notebook: one page for penal convicts, one for those condemned to death. They warn him the night before that there will be someone to comfort the next day at such-and-such a time; he asks what they are, convict or for the scaffold, reads the page over again; then he turns up. And so it is that he gets to meet all those who are headed for Toulon and all those who are headed for La Grève, and they all get to meet him.

Oh! Instead of that, if only they would find me some young curate, any old country priest taken from the first parish they come to; if only they would fetch him from his fireside where he is reading his book and not expecting anything, and say to him:

"There is a man who is going to die, and you must be the one to comfort him. You must be there when they bind his hands, there when they cut his hair; to get into the tumbril with your crucifix to hide the headsman from him; be jolted about on the cobbles with him all the way to La Grève; make your way through the dreadful bloodthirsty mob with him; kiss and embrace him at the foot of the scaffold and stay there until his head is in one place and his body in another."

Let them bring him to me then, all a-quiver, trembling from top to toe; let them thrust me into his arms, at his feet; he will weep, we will weep, he will have meaningful words to say to me and I will be comforted, my heart will grow small and enter his, my soul will be his, and his God will be mine.

But this kind old man, what is he to me? What am I to him? Some wretched individual, another vague shadow among the many he has seen, just another statistic to add to the total number of executions.

Perhaps it was wrong of me to rebuff him like that; he is the good one, me the bad. Sadly it isn't my fault! It is the breath of the condemned man that withers and destroys everything.

They have just brought me something to eat: they thought I must need it. A dainty, carefully chosen spread, what looks like chicken, other things too. Well! I tried to eat, but just one mouthful and I spat it out again, so bitter and noxious did it seem!

31

A GENTLEMAN IN A HAT JUST CAME IN; he barely gave me a glance then opened out a folding foot rule and began measuring the stones in the wall from top to bottom, talking very loudly, one minute saying: "That's it"; the next: "That's not it".

I asked the policeman who it was. Apparently he is some sort of junior architect who works at the prison.

As for me, I aroused his curiosity. He exchanged a few veiled remarks with the turnkey who had come with him; then he stared at me for a moment, shook his head unconcernedly and began to talk at the top of his voice again and take measurements.

When his work was done he came over to me, saying in his booming voice:

"My dear fellow, in six months' time this prison will be much improved."

And his gesture seemed to add:

"It's a shame you won't get the benefit of it."

He was almost smiling. I thought I saw the moment coming when he would start to pull my leg gently, like you do a young bride on her wedding night.

My policeman, an old sweat with stripes, took it on himself to answer:

"Monsieur," he told him, "we don't talk so loudly in a dead man's room."

The architect left.

But me, I was there, like one of the stones he had been measuring.

32

A ND THEN SOMETHING ABSURD HAPPENED. They relieved my kind old policeman, whose hand, ungrateful and selfish as I am, I hadn't even shaken. He was replaced by another one: a man with a low brow, cow's eyes, an ineffectual expression.

Still, I didn't take any notice. Sitting at the table I had my back to the door; I was rubbing my forehead with my hand to try and cool it down, my mind was filled with disturbing thoughts.

A gentle tap on my shoulder made me turn round. It was the new policeman. We were alone together.

This is more or less what he said:

"Criminal, are you a kind man?"

"No," I said.

He seemed taken aback by my abrupt reply. However, he went on hesitantly:

"It's not right to be nasty just for the sake of it."

"Why not?" I retorted. "If that's all you have to say, leave me alone. What are you on about?"

"Excuse me, criminal," he replied. "Just a word. It's this. If you could make a poor man happy and it wouldn't cost you anything, wouldn't you do it?"

I shrugged.

"Have you just escaped from the madhouse or something? You've picked a peculiar place to go looking for happiness. Me, make someone happy!"

He lowered his voice and took on an air of secrecy that didn't suit his stupid face.

"Yes, criminal, yes to happiness, yes to good fortune. All this will come to me from you. It's like this. I'm a poor policeman. The work is hard and the pay is bad. I have my own horse to keep and it ruins me. So I go in for the lottery to make up for it. You have to use a bit of savvy. Up till now all I've been lacking for a win is the right numbers. I look everywhere for a sure thing, but I always pick the wrong ones. I go for seventy-six, it comes out seventy-seven. However much I nurture them my numbers never come up – please, it won't take long now, I've nearly finished – so this is a really good opportunity for me. It seems – beg pardon, criminal – that you're passing on today. It's a known fact that people who die like that can see lottery numbers beforehand. Promise me you'll come tomorrow night. What harm will it do you? Give me three numbers, three good ones. What do you say? – don't worry, I'm not afraid of ghosts – here's my address: Popincourt Barracks, staircase A, number twenty-six at the far end of the corridor. You'll recognize me won't you? – or come tonight even, if that suits you better."

I wouldn't have judged this dolt worthy of an answer if a wild hope hadn't suddenly come to me. In a desperate position like mine there are times when you think you can break a chain with a strand of hair.

"Listen," I said, playing the game as much as anyone can who is about to die, "I can make you richer than a king, help you win millions – on one condition."

He opened his idiotic eyes wide.

"What? What? Anything you want, my dear criminal."

"Instead of three numbers I'll give you four, I promise. Just swap clothes with me."

"Is that all!" he exclaimed, starting to undo his tunic.

I got up from the chair. I watched his every move, heart racing. Already I could already see doors opening at the approach of this police uniform, and the square, the street, the Palais de Justice behind me!

But he turned round hesitantly.

"Oh no! It's not so you can get out of here is it?"

I realized all was lost. But I made one last effort, utterly pointless, utterly insane.

"Of course, but your fortune will be made."

He stopped me:

"Oh no, definitely not! Well fancy! And what about my numbers! For them to be any good you have to be dead."

I sat down again, speechless, abandoning any hope I once had.

33

I CLOSED MY EYES, covered them with my hands to try to forget, to forget the present by going into the past. As I dream, memories of my childhood, my youth come back to me one by one, sweet, tranquil, like islands of flowers in the abyss of dark chaotic thoughts that are swirling round my mind.

I see myself a child again, an innocent laughing schoolboy, shouting, playing, running with my brothers on the broad green path in that wild garden where my early years were spent, part of an old convent overlooked by the leaden tip of the sombre dome of the Val-de-Grâce.

Then four years later there I am again, still a child, but already dreamy and passionate. There is a young girl in the deserted garden.

A young Spanish girl with big eyes and long hair, dark bronzed skin, red lips and rosy cheeks, fourteen years old from Andalusia, called Pepa.

Our mothers told us to run and play together: we went for a walk.

They told us to play and we talked, children of the same age but not the same sex.

Yet not even a year later we were running and fighting together. I quarrelled with Pepita over the best apple on the tree; I hit her because of a bird's nest. She cried; I said: "Serves you right!" and together we went to tell our mothers, who thought that what our top end said was wrong and put our bottom ends right.

Now she leans her arm on mine, and I am full of pride and emotion. We walk slowly, talk softly. She drops her handkerchief; I pick it up for her. Our hands tremble as they touch. She talks to me about the little birds, the star you can see way up there, about the bright red sunset behind the trees, or about her friends at school, her dress and her ribbons. We say innocent things and we both blush. The young girl is now a young woman.

That evening – it was a summer evening – we were beneath the chestnut trees at the bottom of the garden. After one of the long silences that filled our walks she suddenly let go of my arm and said: "Let's run!"

I can still see her: she was all in black, in mourning for her grandmother. She had a childish idea, Pepa became Pepita again, she said: "Let's run!"

She raced off ahead of me with her slender waist like a bumblebee's, her little feet that made her dress ride halfway up her legs. I chased after her, she ran away; now and then the breeze from her running lifted her black cape and I saw her fresh, brown back.

I was beside myself. I caught up with her near the old ruined well; by right of conquest I grabbed her by the belt and made her sit down on a grassy bank; she didn't resist. She was out of breath, laughing. But I was serious, and looked into her dark eyes beneath their dark lashes.

"Sit down," she said. "It's still daylight, let's read. Have you got a book?"

I had the second volume of Spallanzi's *Voyages* with me. I opened it at random, sat beside her, she leant on my shoulder and quietly we both started to read the same page. Before turning the page she always had to wait for me. My mind wasn't as quick as hers.

"Have you finished?" she would ask, when I had barely begun.

Meanwhile our heads rested one against the other, our hair entwined, our breath began to mingle, and then suddenly our mouths.

By the time we felt like reading again there were stars in the sky.

"Oh, Maman, Maman!" she said when we got back. "If only you'd seen how fast we ran!"

I said nothing.

"You're quiet," my mother said to me, "you don't look very happy."

But my heart was in heaven.

It was an evening I will remember for the rest of my life.

The rest of my life!

34

THE HOUR HAS JUST STRUCK. I don't know which one: I can't hear the clock very well. It is as though an organ is playing in my ears; it is the droning of my last thoughts.

At this hour of reckoning as I take refuge in memories, I am horrified to find my crime among them, but I want to repent more. I felt more remorse before I was sentenced; since then it seems my mind has only had room for thoughts of death. But I very much want to repent.

When I dreamt for a moment about my past life, and then came back to the axe blow that in a little while will end it, I shudder as if it were something new. My wonderful childhood! My wonderful youth! A length of cloth of gold whose end is dipped in blood. Between then and now runs a river of blood, the other man's and my own.

If one day people read my story, after so many years of innocence and happiness they wouldn't be able to believe this terrible year, which began with a murder and ends with an execution; it would seem like part of it was missing.

And yet, wretched laws and wretched people, I was not a wicked man!

Oh! To be dying in a few hours' time, and to think that a year ago on a day like this I was free and innocent, going for autumn walks, roaming under the trees, through the leaves!

35

A T THIS VERY MOMENT, not far away from me in the houses around the Palais de Justice and the Place de Grève, and all over Paris, there are men coming and going, reading the paper, thinking about their own affairs; shopkeepers selling; young girls getting their ball gowns ready for this evening; mothers playing with their children!

36

I REMEMBER A DAY when I was a child, going to see the great bell of Notre-Dame.

By the time I got to the stone-and-timber framework of the shaft where the great bell hangs with its clapper, which weighs a thou,* I was already dizzy from climbing the dark spiral staircase, running along the rickety walkway that connects the two towers, from having Paris at my feet.

I walked unsteadily along the loose boards, looking from a distance at the bell that was so well known to the children and people of Paris, noticing not without horror that the overhanging and sloping slate roofs that surrounded the bell were level with my feet. Meanwhile, almost like a bird in flight, I could see the Place de Notre-Dame with people going by as if they were ants.

Suddenly the enormous bell rang, a deep reverberation shook the air making the huge, solid tower sway. The floorboards bounced up and down on the beams. The noise nearly knocked me over; I teetered, almost falling, almost sliding down the sloped tiled roofs. I lay on the boards, terrified, gripped them tightly with both arms, speechless, breathless, with that fearful ringing in my ears and staring at the sheer drop, the square far below where all the lucky, peaceful people were walking about.

Well! It seems like I am still in that bell tower. It's dizzying and dazzling all at once, as if the sound of a bell is shaking the inner cavities of my brain. While around me, from far away across a deep abyss, I see only that unruffled, tranquil life that I left behind and where others are still continuing on their way.

37

THE HÔTEL DE VILLE IS A GRIM-LOOKING EDIFICE.
With its straight and steeply pitched roof, its peculiar little bell tower, its large white clockface, all its storeys with their little pillars, its thousands of windows, its well-trodden stairways, its two archways on the right and the left, it is on the same level as La Grève; dark, dismal, face eaten away with age, and so black that it is even black in bright sunlight.

On execution days it spews policemen from every door, watches the condemned man with every window.

While at night the face of its clock, which marked the occasion, is still lit up on the dark, brooding façade.

38

IT IS QUARTER-PAST ONE.
This is what I feel now:

A sharp pain in my head. Cold shudders running down my spine, my forehead burning. Every time I stand up or lean over it seems as if liquid is washing around inside my head, making my brain pound against the sides of my skull.

I twitch convulsively, and every now and then I drop the pen as if from an electric shock.

My eyes sting as if the room were full of smoke.

My elbows hurt.

Another two hours and forty-five minutes and I will be cured.

39

T HEY SAY IT'S NOTHING, that you don't suffer, that it's a gentle end, that death is much simpler like that.

Oh yes? So what are these death throes that last for six weeks, this death rattle that lasts a whole day? What are the agonies of this irredeemable day that goes by so slowly and yet so fast? What is this ladder of torment that ends at the scaffold?

Apparently that isn't suffering.

Are they not the same convulsions, when the blood drains away drop by drop and the mind shuts down thought by thought?

Besides, are they sure you don't suffer? Who told them that? Has anyone heard of a severed head covered in blood that got up on the edge of the basket and shouted to the crowd: "That didn't hurt!"

Are there any dead people who have come back and thanked them, saying: "It's well designed. Leave it as it is. The mechanism is fine."

Was it Robespierre? Was it Louis XVI?...

No, not at all! Less than a minute, less than a second and the deed is done. If only in their minds, have they ever put themselves in the place of the one who is there when the heavy chopper comes down and bites into flesh, severs nerves, shatters vertebrae... What! Half a second! Any pain is avoided...

Hideous!

40

I T IS EXTRAORDINARY that I keep thinking about the King. However much I do it, however much I shake my head, a voice keeps saying in my ear:

"In this very town, at this very moment and not far from here, in another palace there is another man with guards at his door, a man who is as unique among all the people as you are, except that he is as high up as you are low down. His whole existence, minute by minute, is nothing but glory, grandeur, pleasure, exhilaration. Everywhere around him is love, respect, reverence. The loudest voices speak softly to him, the proudest heads bow down. His eyes see nothing but gold and silk. At this moment he is consulting with ministers who all share his opinion; or thinking about tomorrow's hunt, this evening's ball, confident that every celebration will start on time and leaving the job of organizing his entertainment to others. So! This man is flesh and blood the same as you! And for that awful scaffold to come crashing down this instant, for everything to be returned to you – life, liberty, fortune and family – all he has to do is to pick up a pen and write the seven letters of his name* at the bottom of a piece of paper, or even for his coach simply to pass your tumbril! For he is a good man, he might ask no more than that, it will cost him nothing!"

41

So let us be brave about death, let's seize this dreadful idea with both hands and look it straight in the face. Let's ask it to explain what it is, find out what it wants from us; let's turn it inside out back to front, spell out the mystery and see what lies in store for us beyond the grave.

As soon as my eyes close I think I will see a great brightness, chasms of light where my spirit will journey for ever. I think the sky will light up of its own accord, that the stars will be vague, dark marks in it, that instead of appearing as gold sequins on black velvet as they do to the living, they will look like black dots on a sheet of gold.

Or, pitiful wretch that I am, perhaps it will be a terrible abyss walled in by darkness where I fall continually, watching shapes move about in the shadows.

Or when I wake up after the blow I might find myself on some flat, wet surface, crawling along in the darkness, spinning round like a head rolling. I think a strong wind will blow me along, and that other rolling heads will bump into me here and there. In places there will be pools and streams full of a warm, unfamiliar liquid; everything will be black. When, turning round and round, my eyes look up, all they will see is a shadowy sky whose heavy clouds weigh down on them, and in the deepest depths great archways filled with smoke darker than darkness. And they will see tiny red sparks fluttering in the night, which as they get closer turn into firebirds. This is how it will be for all eternity.

It could also be that on certain dates the dead of La Grève gather on dark winter nights on the square that belongs to them. It will be a pale, blood-soaked crowd, and I will never fail to be among them. There will be no moon, and we will speak softly. The Hôtel de Ville will be there with its moth-eaten façade, its ragged roof, and the clock face that showed mercy to no one. On the square will be hell's guillotine where a devil will execute the executioner. It will be at four o'clock in the morning, and our turn to crowd round.

This is probably how things are. But if these dead do come back, what form do they come back in? What parts of their incomplete, mutilated bodies do they keep? Which do they choose? Which is the ghost, the head or the torso?

Alas! What does death do to our soul? What shape and form does it grant to it? What does it give it, what does it take? Where does it put it? Does it sometimes let it have human eyes so it can look at the world and weep?

Oh! A priest! A priest who knows all this! I want a priest, a crucifix to kiss!

My God, always the same!

42

I ASKED TO BE LEFT ALONE TO SLEEP and threw myself on the bed. What happened was that I had a rush of blood to the head that made me sleep. It was my last sleep of this kind.

I had a dream.

I dreamt it was night. I seemed to be in my study with two or three friends, I don't know which ones.

My wife was in bed in the bedroom, asleep with her child.

My friends and I were talking quietly, and what we were saying frightened us.

Suddenly I thought I heard a noise somewhere in the apartment. An odd, faint noise, hard to identify.

My friends heard it as well. We listened; it was like a lock being turned quietly, a bolt being pulled back without making much noise.

There was something about it that made our blood run cold; we were scared. It was so late at night that we thought burglars might be breaking into the house.

We decided to go and have a look. I got up, I took the candle. One after the other my friends followed me.

We went through the bedroom next door. My wife was asleep with her child.

Then we got to the drawing room. Nothing. The paintings were in their gilt frames on the red wall hangings, not moving. It looked as if the door between the drawing room and the dining room was not in its usual place.

We went into the dining room; we walked right round it. I led the way. The door leading to the stairs was shut, so were the windows. As we got to the stove I saw the linen cupboard was open, and that its door had been swung back across the corner of the room as if to hide it.

This surprised me. We thought there was someone behind the door.

I took hold of the door and went to close the cupboard; it wouldn't budge. Surprised, I pulled harder, it suddenly yielded and we found a little old woman, arms by her sides, eyes closed, standing motionless and as if fixed into the corner of the room.

There was something monstrous about all this, it makes my hair stand on end thinking about it.

I asked the old woman:

"What are you doing here?"

She didn't answer.

I asked her:

"Who are you?"

She didn't answer, didn't move, and kept her eyes shut.

My friends said:

"It's probably the accomplice of the people who broke in intending to get up to no good: they ran off when they heard us coming; she couldn't get away and hid herself here."

I questioned her again, but she stayed mute, motionless, unseeing.

One of us pushed her, she fell over.

She fell straight down like a piece of wood, like something dead.

We pushed her with our feet, and then two of us picked her up and leant her against the wall again. She gave no sign of life. We shouted in her ear, she remained dumb, as if deaf.

In the meantime we were losing our patience, there was anger in our fear. One of the others said to me:

"Hold the candle under her chin."

I held the flaming wick under her chin. She half-opened one eye, an empty, lifeless, terrible and unseeing eye.

I took the flame away and said to her:

"At last! Are you going to answer, you old witch? Who are you?"

Her eye closed again as if by itself.

"Oh no, this is too much!" said the others. "Use the candle again! Again! She's got to say something."

I put the candle flame back under the old woman's chin.

She slowly opened her eyes, looked at each of us in turn, and then suddenly, leaning forwards, she blew out the candle with an icy breath. At that moment I felt three sharp teeth sink into my hand in the darkness.

I woke up shivering, bathed in cold sweat.

The kindly chaplain was sitting at the foot of the bed, reading prayers.

"Have I been asleep for long?" I asked.

"You've been asleep for an hour, my son," he said. "They've brought your child to see you. She's waiting in the next room for you. I didn't want them to wake you."

"Oh!" I cried out. "My daughter, let them bring me my daughter!"

43

S HE IS PURE, rosy, she has big eyes, she is beautiful!
They had put a little dress on her that really suited her.

I picked her up in my arms, sat her on my knee, kissed her hair.

Why wasn't her mother with her? – "Her mother is unwell, so is her grandmother." That's all right.

She looked at me in surprise. Cuddled, embraced, smothered in kisses and allowing me to do it, yet every so often casting an anxious glance towards her nursemaid, who was crying in the corner.

Finally I was able to speak.

"Marie!" I said. "My little Marie!"

I held her tightly to me, my chest heaving with sobs. She gave a little cry.

"Oh, you're hurting me, Monsieur!" she said.

Monsieur! It was nearly a year since she had seen me, the poor child. She had forgotten me – face, voice, accent – besides, who would recognize me with this beard, these clothes, this face drained of colour? What! Wiped from her memory already, the only one in which I wanted to live on! Already not a father! Condemned no longer to hear that word, the one from the language of children, so sweet it can never really be part of the language of adults: *Papa!*

To hear it from this mouth once more, just once, was all I would have asked of the forty years they were taking from me.

"Listen, Marie," I said, clasping her little hands together in mine, "don't you recognize me at all?"

She looked at me with her lovely eyes and answered:

"No I don't!"

"Look harder," I said. "What, you mean you don't know who I am?"

"Oh yes," she said. "You're a gentleman."

Alas! Loving just one person passionately in the whole world, loving them with all your heart and having them there in front of you, seeing you, looking at you, talking to and answering you, and not knowing who you are! Wanting to be comforted by them alone, for them to be the only one not to know that you need this because you are going to die!

"Do you have a papa, Marie?" I went on.

"Yes, Monsieur," the child said.

"So where is he?"

Her big eyes looked up, amazed.

"Oh! You don't know then? He's dead."

Then she gave a cry. I almost dropped her.

"Dead!" I said. "Marie, do you know what it means to be dead?"

"Yes, Monsieur," she answered. "He is in the ground and up in heaven."

Then of her own accord she went on:

"I pray to the Good Lord for him every morning and every night on Maman's knee."

I kissed her forehead.

"Say your prayer for me, Marie."

"I can't, Monsieur. You don't say prayers in the daytime. Come to my house tonight; I'll say it then."

Enough of this. I interrupted her.

"Marie, I'm your papa."

"Oh!" she said.

I added: "Do you want me to be your papa?"

The child turned away.

"No, my papa was much handsomer."

I covered her in tears and kisses. She tried to get out of my arms, crying out:

"Your beard's hurting me."

I took her back on my lap, gazing fondly at her, and asked:

"Can you read, Marie?"

"Yes," she replied. "I'm good at reading. Mama teaches me."

"Come on then, read something," I said, pointing to a piece of paper screwed up in one of her tiny hands.

She shook her pretty head.

"I only know how to read stories."

"Just try. Come on, read."

She opened out the piece of paper and began to spell with her finger:

"W – A – R, war, R – A – N – T, rant... Warrant..."

I snatched it from her hands. She was reading my death sentence. Her nursemaid had bought it for a sou. It was costing me a lot more than that.

There aren't words to describe what I felt. My roughness had frightened her; she was almost in tears. Suddenly she said:

"Give me my piece of paper back! It's for me to play with."

I handed her back to her nanny.

"Take her away."

Then I dropped back into my chair, grim, abandoned, in despair. They will come very soon; I don't care about anything any more; the last shred of feeling in my heart has shattered. I am ready for what they are going to do.

44

THE PRIEST IS A GOOD MAN, so is the policeman. I think they shed a tear when I said to take my child away.

It is over with. Now I must steel myself, fix my mind on the executioner, on the tumbril, the police, the crowds on the bridge, the crowds on the embankment, the crowds at the windows, and on what will be waiting for me on the desolate Place de Grève, which could be paved with all the heads it has seen roll.

I think there is still an hour left for me to get used to all of that.

45

THE WHOLE CROWD WILL LAUGH AND CLAP, applaud. And among all those people who are still free and not known to any jailer, who are running excitedly to see an execution, among that sea of heads which fill the square there will be more than one that is fated to follow mine into the red basket sooner or later. More than one who is going there on my account who will go there on his own.

At a particular place on La Grève there is a predestined spot for these predestined individuals, a centre of attraction, a trap. They circle round and round until they are caught in it.

46

MY LITTLE MARIE! They have taken her back to her games; she is looking out at the crowds from the window of the cab and has already forgotten about the gentleman.

Maybe I still have time to write a few pages for her so she might read them one day, might shed tears for today in fifteen years' time.

Yes, she must hear my story from me, about why the name I am leaving behind for her is covered in blood.

47

MY STORY

[Editor's Note: The pages that were with this one have yet to be found. Perhaps, as those that follow seem to suggest, the condemned man did not have time to write them. It was already late when he thought of it.]

48

FROM A ROOM IN THE HÔTEL DE VILLE.

From the Hôtel de Ville!... So I'm here. The hideous journey is over. The square is there, and beneath the dreadful window is the baying crowd, waiting for me and laughing.

However much I braced myself, however much I clenched my fists, my courage failed me. When, above all the heads I saw those two red shafts with the black triangle at the top, standing between two street lamps on the embankment, my courage failed me. I asked to make one last declaration. They left me and went to fetch a crown prosecutor. I am waiting for him, so that's something at least.

This is it:

Three o'clock struck, they came to tell me it was time. I trembled, as if I hadn't been thinking of anything else for the last six hours, the last six weeks, the last six months. It was as if I wasn't expecting it.

They led me along their corridors, down their staircases. They pushed me between two grilles on the ground floor and into a dark, cramped, vaulted room, barely lit by the light of a wet, misty day. There was a chair in the middle. They told me to sit down; I sat down.

As well as the priest and the policemen there were several people standing by the door and along the walls, and there were also three men.

The first, the tallest and the oldest, was fat and red-faced. He was wearing a frock coat and a misshapen tricorne hat. It was him.

He was the executioner, the servant of the guillotine. The two others were his servants.

I had barely sat down when the other two came up behind me like cats, and suddenly I felt cold steel on my hair, heard the squeaking of scissors.

Cut anyhow, my hair tumbled onto my shoulders in wisps, and the man in the three-cornered hat gently brushed them off with his big hand.

Around me they were talking quietly.

Outside there was a loud noise, like a tremor that rose and breeze. At first I thought it was the river, but from the roars of laughter I could tell it was the crowd.

A young man by the window, who was writing in pencil in a portfolio, asked one of the jailers what they called what they were doing here.

"The washing of the condemned," replied the other.

And I realized it would be in tomorrow's paper.

All of a sudden one of the servants took off my jacket, while the other took my hands, which were at my side, put them behind my back, and I felt the knots of a rope being slowly wound round my wrists. At the same time the other one undid my cravat. My cambric shirt, all I had left of my former self, seemed to make him hesitate for a second; then he began cutting off the collar.

At these terrible precautionary measures, at the sudden chill of steel on my neck, my elbows twitched and I gave muffled howl. The assistant's hand was shaking.

"I'm sorry, Monsieur!" he said. "Did I hurt you?"

Executioners are such gentle people.

Outside the crowds were shouting louder.

The fat man with the pimply face offered me a handkerchief soaked in vinegar to inhale.

"Thank you," I said in the firmest voice I could manage, "there's no need. I feel all right."

Then one of them bent down and tied my ankles using a thin, slack rope which let me take short steps. This rope was attached to the one round my wrists.

Then the fat man slipped my jacket over my shoulders and knotted the sleeves together under my chin. What he had to do here was now done.

The priest came over with his crucifix.

"Come along, my son," he said.

The two servants took hold of me under my arms. I stood up, I walked. My steps were feeble, I sagged as if each of my legs had two knees.

At that moment the double outer doors opened. An almighty clamour, cold air and white light burst in on me in the darkness. From the depths of the dismal little cell I suddenly saw it all at once through the rain, the mass of screaming heads of people packed pell-mell on the banisters of the great staircase of the Palais de Justice; on the right on the same level as the doorway was a line of police horses, only their front legs and chests visible to me because of the low door; opposite, a detachment of soldiers in battle order; to the left, the back of a tumbril with a ladder leaning steeply up against it. A horrifying scene, nicely framed in the doorway of a prison.

This was the dreaded moment for which I had been saving up my courage. I took three steps and appeared at the door of the cell.

"There he is! There he is!" shouted the crowd. "He's coming out at last!"

Those nearest to me clapped their hands. More loudly than for a beloved king.

It was an ordinary tumbril with a scrawny horse and a carter in a blue smock with red patterns on it, like the market gardeners around Bicêtre wear.

The fat man wearing the tricorne hat got in first.

"Hello, Monsieur Sanson!" yelled the children hanging off the railings.

One of the servants followed him.

"Bravo, Mardi!" yelled the children again.

They both sat on the bench seat at the front.

It was my turn. I climbed in quite steadily.

"He's all right!" said a woman standing next to the policemen.

Her dreadful accolade gave me courage. The priest came and sat next to me. They had put me on the bench at the rear with my back to the horse. This last little act of thoughtfulness made me shudder.

They do put compassion into it.

I wanted to look round. Police in front, police behind; then crowds, crowds and crowds; a sea of heads all over the square.

A detachment of mounted police were waiting at the gate in the railings round the Palais de Justice.

The officer gave an order. The tumbril and its retinue set off, as if driven forwards by the shouts of the mob.

We drove out through the railings. As soon as the tumbril turned towards the Pont-au-Change the whole square exploded with noise from the cobbles all the way up to the rooftops, while in response the bridges and embankments made the ground shake.

It was here the waiting detachment joined the escort.

"Hats off! Hats off!" cried a thousand voices as one – as if for the King.

I gave a horrible laugh too, and said to the priest:

"Their hats, my head."

We went at walking pace.

On the Quai aux Fleurs the air was full of sweet smells: it was market day. The flower girls had left their stalls to come and see me.

Opposite, just before the square tower on the corner of the Palais de Justice there were little inns whose entresols were full of spectators delighted to have such good seats. Especially the women. It was a good day for the innkeepers.

There were tables, chairs, scaffolding and carts for hire. Everything groaned under the weight of spectators. Pedlars of human blood shouted at the top of their voices:

"Who wants a seat?"

I was seized with fury with these people. I longed to shout out to them:

"Who wants mine?"

Meanwhile the tumbril kept moving. With every yard it went the crowd broke up behind it, and with distraught eyes I watched it close up again back along my route.

As we got to the Pont-au-Change I glanced over my right shoulder. My gaze settled on the far embankment where, above the houses, there was a solitary dark tower covered in sculptures, at the top of which I could see two stone monsters sat sideways on. For some reason I asked the priest what the tower was called.

"Saint-Jacques-la-Boucherie," said the executioner.

I don't know why but in the mist, despite the pale, fine drizzle that traced through the air like the strands of a spider's web, I didn't miss a thing that was going on around me. Every detail was a new source of torment. No words can describe my feelings.

Halfway across the Pont-au-Change, so wide and packed with people that we could barely make our way through, I was suddenly seized with terror. I was afraid I would faint – the final vanity! So I made myself blind and deaf to everything except the priest, whose words, interspersed by the rumble of the crowd, I could barely hear.

I grabbed the crucifix and kissed it.

"Have mercy on me, O my God!" I said. And I tried hard to lose myself in this thought.

But every jolt of the rough tumbril shook me around. Then suddenly I felt terribly cold. The rain had soaked through my clothes and was making my head wet where my hair had been cut short.

"Are you shivering with cold, my son?" asked the priest.

"Yes," I answered.

Sadly not just with cold!

At the bend in the bridge women took pity on me because I was so young.

We headed along the fateful embankment. I began to not see or hear anything. All these voices, all these heads at the windows, in doorways, at the shutters of shops, on the brackets of the streetlamps; these cruel, eager onlookers; this crowd who all knew who I was while I didn't know any of them; this road paved and walled with human faces... I was drunk, dazed, senseless. It was unbearable to have the weight of so many eyes bearing down on you.

I swayed about on the seat, not even taking any notice of the priest or the crucifix any more.

In the clamour all around me I could no longer tell cries of pity from shouts of delight, laughter from groans, voices from noises; it was all just a buzzing in my head, like an echo in a cooking pot.

Unthinkingly my eyes read the shop signs.

At one point I was seized with a bizarre curiosity to turn round and see where I was going. It was my mind's last act of bravado. But my body didn't want to; my neck was paralysed as if in anticipation of death.

Across the river to my left all I could make out was the tower of Notre-Dame, which seen from there hid the other one. It was the one with the flagpole. There were a lot of people, they must have had a good view.

And the tumbril drove on and on, the shops went by, their signs came one after the other, handwritten, painted, gilt, and the mob laughed and stamped their feet in the mud, and I let myself go as a sleeper gives himself up to a dream.

Suddenly the line of shops that my eyes were fixed on ended abruptly at the edge of a square. The voice of the crowd became more strident and yelping, even more cheerful. The tumbril suddenly stopped and I nearly fell face down on the boards. The priest held me up. "Be brave!"

he whispered. Then a ladder was brought to the back of the tumbril; he gave me his arm, I climbed down, I took a step, I turned round to take another, but I couldn't. Between two streetlamps on the embankment I saw something sinister.

Oh! It was all real!

I stopped, as if already reeling under the blow.

"I have a last declaration to make!" I cried out, weakly.

They brought me up here.

I asked them to let me write down my last wishes. They untied my hands, but the rope is here, ready, and all the rest is down there.

49

SOME SORT OF JUDGE, a commissioner, a magistrate, I don't know what, has just arrived. Hands clasped, I went down on my knees and asked him for a pardon. With an inevitable smile he asked if that was all I had to say.

"A pardon, a pardon!" I repeated. "Or another five minutes, for mercy's sake!"

"Who knows? Maybe it will come. It's terrible to die like this at my age! It often happens, pardons can come at the last minute. And who is there to pardon, Monsieur, if not me?"

The loathsome executioner! He went up to the judge and said the execution had to be done at a particular time, that it was almost that time, that he was responsible, and besides it was raining and it might go rusty.

"Oh for pity's sake! Just one minute to wait for my pardon! Or I'll put up a fight! I'll bite!"

The judge and the executioner went out. I'm alone. Alone with two policemen.

Oh, that terrible crowd, laughing like hyenas! Who knows if I'll escape their clutches, if I'll be saved? If my pardon?... It's not possible I won't be pardoned!

Oh, the villains! It sounds as if they are coming up the stairs...

FOUR O'CLOCK

*Claude Gueux**

THE LETTER BELOW, the original of which is lodged at the offices of the *Revue de Paris,* does its author too much credit for us not to reproduce it here. From now on it will be included in every reprint of *Claude Gueux.*

Dunkerque, 30th July 1834

To the Editor of the Revue de Paris
Dear Sir,
Claude Gueux, *by Victor Hugo, which you published in your issue of the 6th instant, offers us a great lesson; please help me to make it of benefit.*

Please be so kind as to have printed, at my expense, as many copies as there are deputies in France, and to send one to each of them personally.

With respectful greetings,

Charles Carlier
Merchant

Seven or eight years ago a man called Claude Gueux, a poor working man, was living in Paris. With him were a young woman, his mistress, and a child by this young woman. I am telling things as they are, leaving the reader to gather any moral lessons that the facts may sow along the wayside. This working man was capable, skilled, intelligent, had been dealt a bad hand by the education system and a good hand by nature, being unable to read but able to think. One winter work was hard to come by. No fire, nothing to eat in their garret. The man, the young woman and the child were cold and hungry. The man stole. I don't know what he stole or where he stole it from. What I do know is that the outcome of this theft was three days' food and heat for the woman and child and five years' prison for the man.

The man was sent to serve his time at Clairvaux prison. Clairvaux, an abbey that had been turned into a fortress, monks' cells turned into prison cells, an altar turned into a stocks. When we talk of progress, this is how some people understand and put it into practice. This is what they use our word to describe.

Let us continue.

When he arrived he was put in a dungeon at night and a workshop during the day. It is not the workshop I blame.

Claude Gueux, until recently an honest working man but now a thief, was a dignified, solemn character. He had a lofty brow, already furrowed despite the fact he was still young, a few grey hairs hidden among his thick black locks, mild but strong eyes deep-set beneath well-sculpted eyebrows, flared nostrils, a rolling chin, a scornful upper lip. It was a handsome face. We will see what society did with it.

He spoke little, being more inclined to use gestures, and there was something authoritative about him which made people do what he said, his thoughtful manner, one of seriousness rather than suffering. Yet he had undoubtedly suffered.

In the jail where Claude Gueux was imprisoned there was a workshop manager, a form of civil servant peculiar to prisons, a combination of jailer and tradesman whose word was a command to the worker at the same time as being a threat to the prisoner, who put tools in your hand and shackles on your feet. This individual was a particular variety of the species, a gruff man, dictatorial, governed by his own ideas, constantly held in check by his sense of personal authority; admittedly good company on occasions, magnanimous, even jolly, and with the good grace to laugh and joke; harsh rather than firm; not about to be prevailed upon by anyone, not even himself; no doubt a good father, a good husband, but out of duty rather than virtue – in a word, not malicious, just unpleasant. He was one of those people without passion or flexibility who are made up of lifeless molecules, who greet the spark of any new idea, any contact with human feelings, with dull indifference, who have icy rages, dismal dislikes, lose their temper without showing emotion, who flare up without getting heated, whose calorific content is non-existent, and who you would think were made of wood; they burn at one end but are cold at the other.* Part and parcel of this man's character was persistence. He was proud of being persistent and likened himself to Napoleon. This is nothing but an optical illusion. A lot of people are fooled by this and, from a distance, take persistence for will power, a candle flame for a star. So, once this man had directed what he called his will power at some ludicrous thing, he barged through every obstacle with a clear conscience until that ludicrous thing was completed. Stubbornness without intelligence is an adjunct to stupidity, and serves to compound it. It goes a long way. Generally when some private or public disaster comes crashing down on us, if we investigate, judging from the debris lying all around, how it was assembled in the first place, we nearly always discover that it was blindly engineered by some second-rate and obstinate man who believed in and admired himself. There are a great many of these stubborn, deadly little people all over the world who think themselves guardian angels.

So this was what he was, the workshop manager at Clairvaux prison. This was the stuff the flint was made of that society used to strike prisoners every day to get a spark from them.

The sparks that flints like this draw from stones like those often start fires.

We have already said that as soon as he arrived at Clairvaux, Claude Gueux was assigned to a workshop and put to work. The workshop manager got to know him, saw he was a good worker and treated him well. One day, being in a good mood and seeing that Claude Gueux was unhappy, because this man was always thinking about what he called his wife, he apparently told him, in a convivial fashion and to pass the time as well as cheer him up, that the wretched woman had become a working girl. Coldly, Claude asked what had happened to the child. This wasn't known.

After a few months Claude adapted to prison life and seemed not to think about anything any more. A particular brand of austere calmness peculiar to his character reasserted itself.

More or less during this same period Claude had built up a remarkable influence over his fellow prisoners. As if by some unspoken agreement, and without anyone knowing why, not even him, all the men asked his advice, listened to him, admired and imitated him, which is the sincerest form of flattery. It was no mean achievement to be obeyed by so many naturally disobedient people. This authority came to him without him even thinking about it. It was due to the look in his eye. A man's eyes are a window through which we see thoughts coming and going inside his head.

Put a man with ideas among men who have none and, by some irresistible law of attraction, after a certain time all these darkened minds will gravitate humbly and adoringly towards the illuminated mind. Some men are iron and others are magnets. Claude was a magnet.

So in less than three months Claude became the heart and soul, the law and order of the workshop. He was the clock face around which they, the hands, revolved. There must have been times when he himself wondered if he was king or captive. He was a sort of prisoner pope with his cardinals.

And, due to a totally natural reaction whose effects were felt at every level, being loved by the prisoners he was hated by the jailers. This is how it always is. Popularity never comes without dislike. The love of the slaves is always exceeded by the hatred of the masters.

Claude Gueux was a big eater. It was a distinctive feature of his constitution. His stomach was so made that the food for two men was barely enough to last him a day. Signor de Cotadilla* had an appetite like that and used to laugh about it; but what gives a Spanish grandee with five hundred thousand sheep cause to be cheerful is a burden for a working man and an ordeal for a prisoner.

Free in his attic, Claude Gueux used to work all day, earn his daily bread of four pounds and eat it. In prison, Claude Gueux worked all day and was invariably given a pound and a half of bread and four ounces of meat for his trouble. The ration never varied. So Claude Gueux was normally hungry in Clairvaux prison.

He was hungry, just that. He didn't talk about it. That was how he was.

One day Claude had just wolfed down his meagre crust and had gone back to work, thinking to get the better of hunger that way. The other prisoners were eating away in good heart. A pale, weak-looking young man came over and stood by him. In his hand was his ration, which he hadn't touched, and a knife. He stood next to Claude, looking as if he wanted to speak to him but daren't. This man with his bread and meat bothered Claude.

"What do you want?" he snapped eventually.

"For you to do me a favour," said the young man, nervously.

"What?" Claude retorted.

"For you to help me eat this. I've had too much."

A tear trickled from Claude's proud eyes. He took the knife, divided the young man's ration into two equal parts, took one of them and began to eat.

"Thank you," said the young man. "If you want we can share it like this every day."

"What's your name?" said Claude Gueux.

"Albin."

"Why are you here?" Claude went on.

"For stealing."

"Me too," said Claude.

And in fact they did share like this every day. Claude Gueux was thirty-six, although so stern was his normal manner of thinking there were times when he seemed fifty. Albin was twenty – you would have said seventeen: there was still so much innocence in this thief's eyes. A close friendship developed between the two men – more of a father-son relationship than brotherly. Albin was still almost a child; Claude was nearly an old man already.

They worked in the same workshop, they slept in the same part of the dormitory, they exercised in the same yard, they ate the same food. Each of the two friends was the whole world for the other. They seemed happy.

We have already talked about the workshop manager. Hated by the prisoners, to make them obey him the man often had no choice but to turn to Claude, who was loved by them. On more than one occasion when he needed to prevent a revolt or a riot from breaking out, Claude's informal authority had come to the aid of the manager's official authority. In fact, to control the prisoners ten words from Claude were worth the same number of policemen. Claude had helped the manager out like this many times. So the manager cordially disliked him. He envied this thief. In his heart of hearts he harboured a private, jealous, unrelenting hatred for Claude, the hatred of the rightful sovereign for the actual sovereign, of worldly power for spiritual power.

Hatreds like that are the worst.

Claude was very fond of Albin and didn't take the workshop manager into account.

One morning, as the convicts were walking in pairs from the dormitory to the workshop, one of the jailers called to Albin, who was with Claude, and told him the manager was asking for him.

"What does he want with you?" said Claude.

"I don't know," said Albin.

The jailer took Albin away.

The morning went by; Albin didn't come back to the workshop. When it was mealtime Claude thought he would meet up with Albin in the exercise yard. Albin wasn't in the yard. They went back to the workshop; Albin didn't reappear there. The whole day passed like that. That evening as the prisoners were being taken back to the dormitory, Claude looked round for Albin but couldn't see him. He seemed to be in great pain at that moment because he spoke to a jailer, something he never did.

"Is Albin sick?" he asked.

"No," answered the jailer.

"So how come he hasn't come back today?" Claude went on.

"Ah!" said the turnkey offhandedly. "That's because he's been moved to another section."

Witnesses who later testified to these events noticed that when he heard the jailer's reply, Claude's hand, in which he had a lit candle, trembled slightly. He went on calmly:

"Who gave that order?"

The jailer replied:

"M.M."

The workshop manager was called M.M.

The next day went by like the one before, without Albin.

That evening when work was finished, M.M. did his usual rounds of the workshop. When Claude saw him coming he took off his thick woollen cap and did up his grey jacket, the dismal uniform of Clairvaux, since it is an accepted dictum in prison that a respectfully buttoned jacket is regarded favourably by superiors, and stood with his cap in his hand at the end of the workbench waiting for the manager to come by. The manager came past.

"Monsieur!" said Claude.

The workshop manager stopped and half turned.

"Monsieur," Claude went on, "is it true that Albin has been moved to a another section?"

"Yes," answered the manager.

"Monsieur," Claude went on, "I need Albin so I can live."

And he added:

"You know I don't get enough to eat with the prison ration, and that Albin shares his food with me."

"That's up to him," said the manager.

"Monsieur, isn't there any way of getting Albin put back in the same section as me?"

"Impossible. The decision has been made."

"Who by?"

"Me."

"Monsieur M.," Claude went on, "it's a matter of life and death for me, and it depends on you."

"I never go back on a decision."

"Monsieur, have I done something to you? What have I done?"

"Nothing."

"Then why separate me from Albin?" said Claude.

"Because," said the manager.

And with that explanation the manager walked blithely on.

Claude looked down at his feet and did not reply. A poor lion in its cage, whose dog has been taken away from him.

We have to say here that despondency over this separation did nothing to spoil what could be described as the prisoner's pathologically voracious appetite. Neither did anything about him seem to change noticeably. He didn't talk about Albin to any of his fellow prisoners. At exercise time he walked in the yard by himself and was hungry. Nothing more.

Yet those who knew him well noticed something dark and ominous spreading across his face more and more each day. Not only that, he was more gentle than ever.

Several of them offered to share their rations with him, but with a smile he refused.

Every evening after being given this explanation by the workshop manager he did something insane that was surprising in such a serious man. When at the set time the manager came to do his usual tour of inspection and walked past Claude's workbench, Claude looked up and stared him straight in the eye, then said in a voice filled with despair and anger which had something of both a plea and a threat about it, just these two words: "And Albin?" The manager either pretended not to hear or walked off with a shrug.

The man was wrong to shrug. Because to everyone who witnessed these odd scenes it was clear that Claude Gueux had quietly made up his mind to do something. The whole prison waited anxiously to see what the outcome would be of this conflict between persistence and resolve.

It was noted on at least one occasion that Claude told the workshop manager:

"Listen, Monsieur, give me my friend back. You will be doing a good thing, I assure you. Note that I am telling you this."

Another time, a Sunday, he was sitting on a rock in the yard, elbows on his knees, head in his hands and not having moved from this position for several hours, when a convict called Faillette went up to him with a laugh and shouted:

"What the hell are you doing, Claude?"

Claude looked up slowly, stern-faced, and said:

"*I'm judging someone.*"

Eventually, on the evening of 25th October 1831, as the manager was doing his rounds, Claude crushed a watch glass loudly under his foot which he had found that morning in one of the corridors. The manager asked where the noise came from.

"It's nothing," said Claude. "It's me. Give me Albin back, Monsieur, give me my friend back."

"Impossible," said the master.

"Nonetheless you must," said Claude in a quiet, firm voice and, looking the manager straight in the face, he added:

"Think about it. Today is the 25th of October. I will give you till the 4th of November."

One of the jailers pointed out to M.M. that Claude was threatening him, which was grounds for solitary confinement.

"No," said the manager, smiling contemptuously. "No solitary confinement. We have to be kind to these people!"

The next day a convict called Pernot came over to Claude, who was walking by himself, deep in thought, leaving the other prisoners to their larks in a small patch of sunshine at the other end of the courtyard.

"Hey, Claude! What's on your mind? You look sad."

"*I'm afraid,*" said Claude, "*that some misfortune might soon befall that good M.M. of ours.*"

There are nine days between 25th October and 4th November. Claude didn't let a single one of them go by without warning the workshop manager about the increasingly distressed state that Albin's departure was putting him in. Once, tiring of this, the manager gave him twenty-four hours' solitary confinement, because the request sounded too much like a warning. This was all Claude received.

The 4th of November came. Claude woke with a calm expression that no one had seen since the day M.M.'s *decision* had separated him from his friend. When he got up he rummaged around in a sort of deal box at the foot of the bed, which contained his few poor possessions. He took out a pair of dressmaker's scissors. Along with a damaged copy of *Émile* it was all he had left of the woman he had loved, the mother of his child, and of his once happy little household. These two objects were of no use to Claude: the scissors could only be used by a woman, the book by someone educated. Claude could neither sew nor read.

As he walked through the disgraced former cloisters, now white-washed, which were used as a covered walk in winter, he went up to a prisoner called Ferrari who was staring at the heavy bars on one of the windows. In his hand Claude had the small pair of scissors; he showed them to Ferrari and said:

"This evening I'm going to cut those bars with these scissors."

Disbelieving, Ferrari began to laugh, as did Claude.

That morning he worked even more enthusiastically than usual; never had he done things so quickly or so well. He seemed to set particular store on spending the morning finishing a straw hat which a respectable gentleman from Troyes, a Monsieur Bressier, had paid him for in advance.

Shortly before midday he found an excuse to go down to the carpenters' workshop on the ground floor, just below his own. Claude was as well liked there as everywhere else, but he rarely went in the place. So:

"Well! It's Claude!"

They gathered round him. It was cause for celebration. Claude gave a quick glance round the room. None of the warders was there.

"Who's got an axe I can borrow?" he said.

"What for?" they asked.

He replied:

"To kill the workshop manager this evening."

They offered him several axes to choose from. He took the smallest, which was extremely sharp, hid it down his trousers then left. There were twenty-seven prisoners there. He didn't ask any of them to keep it a secret. They all did.

They didn't even talk about it among themselves.

Individually they all just waited to see what would happen. It was a dreadful business, simple and straightforward. No likely complications. It wasn't possible to offer Claude advice, or to betray him.

An hour later in the covered walk he went up to a sixteen-year-old convict who was yawning and told him he should learn to read. Just then a prisoner called Faillette stopped Claude and asked what the hell he had hidden down his trousers. Claude said:

"An axe to kill M.M. with this evening."

Then he added:

"Can you see it?"

"Only just," said Faillette.

The rest of the day went by as normal. At seven in the evening the prisoners were locked back in, each group in their particular workshop, and as was apparently usual the warders left them alone in there, only coming back after the manager's rounds.

So Claude Gueux was locked in his workshop like the rest of his fellow craftsmen.

And then an extraordinary scene took place in the workshop, a scene not without grandeur or horror, and of a kind that no history book could tell.

As the judicial inquiry that took place later noted, there were eighty-two thieves there including Claude.

Once the warders had left them on their own, Claude stood up on his bench and told the whole room that he had something to say. Everyone went quiet.

Then Claude spoke up:

"You all know Albin was my brother. I don't get enough to eat with what they give me here. Even if I bought food with the little I earn it wouldn't be enough. Albin used to share his ration with me; at first I loved him because he gave me something to eat, but then because he loved me. The workshop manager, M.M., separated us. Us being together did him no harm, but he's a wicked man who takes pleasure in tormenting people. I've asked him for Albin again and again. You saw, didn't you? He didn't want to. I gave him till the fourth of November to let me have Albin back. He had me put in solitary for saying that. During this time I have judged him, and I have condemned him to death. Today is the fourth of November. In two hours' time he'll be coming to do his rounds. I'm letting you know that I'm going to kill him. Do you have anything to say?"

No one said a word.

So Claude went on. It seems he spoke with remarkable eloquence, something that came naturally to him in any case. He said he was well aware that he was about to commit an act of violence, but he didn't think he was in the wrong. He appealed to the consciences of the eighty-two thieves who were listening to bear witness:

That he was in dire necessity;

That being forced to take the law into your own hands was a blind alley down which you sometimes found yourself headed;

That in all honesty he couldn't take the manager's life without giving his own, but he felt it was a good thing to give your life for something just;

That he had given this, and nothing but this, considerable thought for two months;

That he genuinely believed he wasn't letting himself be carried away by feelings of resentment, although if that were the case he begged them to tell him so;

That he was putting forward his reasons in an honest way to the fair-minded men around him;

That he was therefore going to kill M.M., but if anyone had any objections he was prepared to listen to them.

Only one voice was raised, saying that before he killed the works manager Claude should try one last time to talk to him and sway him.

"Fair point," said Claude, "I'll do that."

The great clock struck eight. The works manager was coming at nine.

Once this bizarre court of appeal had so to speak confirmed the sentence he had passed, Claude calmed down again. He put all the underwear and clothing he owned, a prisoner's poor cast-offs, on a table, and then, calling over those of his fellow inmates who he liked most after Albin one by one, he shared it out between them. All he kept was the little pair of scissors.

Then he kissed and embraced them all. Some were crying, and for them he had a smile.

There were moments during this final hour when he talked so calmly, even cheerfully, that more than one of his friends inwardly hoped, as they later admitted, that he might go back on his decision. At one point he even amused himself by blowing down his nose to snuff out one of the few candles that lit the workshop, because there were still bad habits from his upbringing that got the better of his natural dignity more often than they should. Nothing could quite wash the smell of the Paris gutter from this former street urchin.

He saw a young convict who had gone pale, and who was staring at him and trembling, probably because of what he was about to see.

"Come on, cheer up young man!" Claude said to him gently, "it'll only take a moment."

When he had shared out all his old clothes, said all his goodbyes, shaken every hand, he went round and broke up a few worried conversations that were going on in various dark corners of the workshop, then told everyone to get back to work. Without a word they all did so.

The workshop where all this took place was an oblong room, rectangular with windows in its two long sides and doors at either end facing each other. The workbenches ran along either side by the windows, the benches at right angles against the wall, with the empty space between the two rows of benches making a kind of corridor that ran all the way down the room from door to door. It was along this long, fairly narrow corridor that the works manager would walk when he did his inspection; he would come in through the south door and leave by the north, having looked at the workers on each side. Usually he went through quite quickly and without stopping.

Claude went back to his bench and got on with his work, like Jacques Clément* went back to praying.

Everyone waited. The moment was approaching. Suddenly they heard the clock strike. Claude said:

"It's quarter to."

Then he stood up, walked solemnly across the room and leant on the corner of the first workbench on the left, just inside the entrance. The expression on his face was perfectly calm and good-natured.

Nine o'clock struck. The door opened. The workshop manager came in.

At that moment you could have heard a pin drop.

As usual the manager was alone.

In he came with his jolly face, self-satisfied and implacable, not seeing Claude standing to the left of the door with his right hand down his trousers, and walked quickly past the first workbenches, nodding, making the odd curt remark, giving the usual routine glances here and there, not noticing that all eyes around him were fastened on a single terrifying thought.

All of a sudden he swung round, surprised to hear footsteps behind him.

It was Claude, who had been following him for the last few moments without a word.

"What are *you* doing?" said the manager. "Why aren't you in your place?"

Because here, a man is no longer a man. He is a dog. He is spoken to as if he were a dog.

Claude answered respectfully:

"There is something I need to speak to you about, Monsieur."

"What?"

"Albin."

"Again!" said the manager.

"As always!" said Claude.

"Really!" the manager went on. "Wasn't twenty-four hours in solitary confinement enough for you?"

Still following him, Claude replied:

"Monsieur, give me my friend back."

"Impossible."

"Monsieur," said Claude in a voice that would have melted the Devil's heart, "I'm begging you, put Albin back with me and you'll see how well I work. You are free, it's all the same to you, you don't know what a friend really is – but me, all I have is four prison walls. You can come and go, can't you – but me, all I've got is Albin. Give him back to me. Albin used to feed me, you know that. All it will cost you is the effort of saying yes. What's it to you if there's one man called Claude Gueux in the workshop and another called Albin? Because it's a simple as that. Monsieur, good, kind Monsieur M., I'm begging you, for Heaven's sake!"

Claude had perhaps never said so much to a jailer all at once. After his exertions he waited, exhausted. With an impatient gesture the manager retorted:

"Impossible. And that's that. Don't mention it to me again, do you hear? You're getting on my nerves."

And since he was in a hurry he walked off quickly. So did Claude. As they were talking they had almost reached the way out. The eighty thieves watched and listened, on tenterhooks.

Gently, Claude took hold of the manager's coat tail.

"I should at least know why I've been condemned to death! Tell me why you've separated me from him?"

"I've already told you," answered the manager. "Because."

And, turning his back on Claude, he reached for the door handle to leave.

Hearing the manager's reply, Claude took a step back. The eighty human statues saw his right hand appear from his trousers holding the axe. The hand was raised and, before the manager could cry out, three axe blows, all in the same place, a hideous thing to describe, had cut his skull wide open. As he fell back a fourth blow gashed into his face. Then, as if in an unstoppable fit of rage, Claude sliced open his right thigh with a needless fifth blow. The workshop manager was dead.

Then Claude threw down the axe and shouted: "*Now the other one!*" The other one was him. They saw him take "his wife's" little scissors from his jacket, and before anyone could think of stopping him he had plunged them into his chest. But the blade was short, his chest deep. He stabbed more than twenty times, screaming: "Damn heart, where are you?" Eventually he collapsed in a pool of blood and passed out on top of the dead man.

Of these two, which was the victim?

When Claude came round he was in bed, covered in sheets and bandages and surrounded by tender care. As well as Sisters of Charity at his bedside there was an investigating magistrate who was drawing up a formal document, and who asked him with great interest: "*How are you feeling?*"

He had lost a lot of blood, but the scissors he had turned on himself with such a touching show of faith hadn't done their job properly; none of the injuries he inflicted on himself were serious. The only wounds that were fatal to him were the ones he had given M.M.

The cross-examinations began. He was asked if it was him who killed the works manager at Clairvaux prison. He answered: "*Yes.*" He was asked why. He replied: "*Because.*"

In the meantime his wounds turned septic. He went down with a nasty fever that almost killed him.

November, December, January and February went by with treatment and preparations. Doctors and judges danced attendance on Claude. One group tended his injuries while the other built his scaffold.

To cut a long story short, on 16th March 1832, now fully recovered, he appeared before the Crown Court in Troyes. Everybody that the town could muster by way of a crowd was there.

Claude bore himself well in court. He had had himself properly shaved, wore no hat and the drab suit of clothes of a prisoner at Clairvaux, each half a different shade of grey.

The crown prosecutor had filled the courtroom with armed troops, "in order", he told those present in court, "to control all the villains who are going to appear as witnesses in this case".

When it came to starting the proceedings there was an unusual hitch. None of the witnesses of the events of 4th November wanted to give evidence against Claude. The presiding judge threatened to use his discretionary powers against them. But to no avail. So Claude told them to testify. All tongues were loosened. They said what they had seen.

Claude listened very carefully to all of them. Whenever one of them failed to mention, either by an oversight or out of fondness for Claude, facts that were imputed against the accused, Claude set the record straight.

Witness by witness the sequence of events that we described earlier unfolded before the court.

There was a point where all the women wept. The court usher called the convict Albin. It was his turn to testify. The police weren't able to stop him throwing himself into Claude's arms. Claude held him, and said to the crown prosecutor with a smile: "This is the villain who shares his food with those who are hungry." Then he kissed Albin's hand.

Once every witness had been heard, the worshipful crown prosecutor got up and began to speak along these lines: "Gentlemen of the jury, society would be shaken to its foundations if those guilty of serious crimes such as this were beyond the reach of prosecution and conviction, etc."

After this memorable discourse, Claude's lawyer spoke. The prosecution and the defence then took it in turns to follow the lines that it is their wont to follow in that particular form of circus known as a criminal trial.

Claude felt that not everything had been said. When his turn came he got up. He spoke in such a way that any intelligent person present would have come away astonished. This poor working man seemed to be more orator than murderer. He spoke standing, in a penetrating and restrained voice and with a frank, honest, determined expression, his gestures rarely varying yet full of authority. He told things as they were, simply, conscientiously, without exaggerating or making light of them, admitted everything, looked Article 296* straight in the face and offered up his neck to it. He had moments of genuine eloquence that moved the crowd, when people in the public gallery repeated his words to each other in whispers. During these murmurings Claude had time to get his breath back, glancing round proudly at those present. At other times this man who couldn't read was as mild, polite and refined as an educated person; while at still others he was modest, moderate, attentive, took the irksome parts of the argument step by step, behaved graciously to the judges. Only once did he give in to an angry outburst. In the speech we quoted, the crown prosecutor had shown that Claude Gueux had murdered the workshop manager without any assault or act of violence on the manager's part, and therefore *without provocation.*

"What!" cried Claude. "I wasn't provoked? Oh yes of course, that's right! I see. A drunk punches me, I kill him, I was provoked, you pardon me, send me to the galleys. But a man who isn't drunk, who's in his right mind, crushes my deepest feelings underfoot for four years, humiliates me for four years, goads me every day, every hour, every minute with a pinprick where I least expect it for four years! I had a wife for whom I stole, he torments me with that wife; I had a child for whom I stole, he torments me with that child; I don't have enough food, a friend gives me some, he takes away my food and my friend. I keep asking him for my friend back, he puts me in solitary confinement. I speak to him respectfully, this stool pigeon, while he talks to me with disdain. I tell him I'm suffering, he tells me I get on his nerves. What do you expect me to do? I kill him. All right, I'm a monster. I killed the man, I wasn't provoked, you cut my head off. Do it!"

A magnificent reaction in our opinion, and one which suddenly revealed, from beneath the system of material provocation on which the disproportionate scale of mitigating circumstances rests, a whole new theory of mental provocation that the law has forgotten.

Once the hearing was over, the presiding judge gave his impartial, enlightening summing-up. This was what came out of it: a bad life. A monster indeed. Claude Gueux began by cohabiting with a woman of ill repute, then stole, then killed. All this was true.

Before sending the jury out to consider their verdict, the judge asked the accused if he had anything to say about the case against him as it stood.

"Not much," Claude replied. "But here it is anyway. I'm a thief and a murderer. I stole and I killed. But why did I steal? Why did I kill? Ask yourselves those two questions, gentlemen of the jury."

After a quarter of an hour's deliberation, following the verdict of the twelve citizens of Champagne who were referred to as *gentlemen of the jury*, Claude Gueux was condemned to death.

There is no doubt that at the very beginning of the proceedings several of them had noticed that the defendant was called *Gueux*,* something which made a deep impression on them.

The sentence was read out to Claude, who simply said:

"*Very well. But why did this man steal? Why did this man kill? These are two questions which they haven't answered.*"

When he got back to prison he ate his supper cheerfully and said:

"Thirty-six years' worth of facts."

He didn't want to appeal. In tears, one of the nuns who had looked after him begged him to do so. So out of kindness to her he made an appeal. He apparently resisted it until the last moment, because when he signed his appeal in the register in the Clerk of the Court's office, the official deadline of three days had expired a few minutes beforehand. Out of gratitude the poor young woman gave him five francs. He took it and thanked her.

While awaiting the outcome of his appeal, the other prisoners at Troyes, who were all devoted to him, offered to help him escape. The convicts threw a nail, a length of wire and the handle of a bucket into his cell through the high barred window. For a man as intelligent as

Claude, any of these things would have been enough to file through his chains. He handed in the handle, the wire and the nail to the jailer.

On 8th June 1832, seven months and four days after the event, the time of atonement came, *pede claudo** as we can see. At seven o'clock that morning the Clerk of the Court came to Claude's cell and informed him that he had only an hour to live. His appeal had been rejected.

"Oh right," said Claude coldly, "and I slept well last night, without suspecting that I'll sleep even better tonight."

It seems that the approach of death always gives the words of strong men particular grandeur.

The priest came, then the executioner. He was humble with the priest, meek with the other. He didn't deny them his body or his soul.

He retained his independence of thought. As they were cutting his hair, in a corner of the cell someone was talking about the cholera epidemic that was threatening Troyes at the time.

"I've nothing to fear from cholera, me," said Claude with a smile.

He also listened very carefully to the priest, admitting many sins and regretting that he hadn't had a religious education.

At his request they had given him back the scissors that he used on himself. One of the blades, which had broken off in his chest, was missing. He asked the jailer to give them to Albin. He also said he would like them to add his food ration for the day to this bequest.

He asked the men who tied his hands to put the five-franc piece that the nun gave him in his right hand, all that he had left now.

At quarter to eight he came out of the prison with the mournful procession that always accompanies a condemned man. He was on foot, pale, eyes fixed on the priest's crucifix, but walking steadily.

They had chosen this particular day for the execution because it was market day, so there would be as many people as possible to see him go past, since there are apparently still semi-primitive towns and villages in France where they take pride in it when society kills a man.

He climbed solemnly onto the scaffold, eyes still fixed on Christ's tree. He wanted to kiss the priest and then the executioner, thanking one and forgiving the other. According to one account the executioner "gently pushed him away".* As the assistant tied him onto the monstrous apparatus he gestured to the priest to take the five-franc piece from his right hand, and said to him:

"*For the poor.*"

As eight o'clock was just striking, the sound from the clock tower drowned out his voice, and his confessor replied that he couldn't hear. Claude waited for the pause between two strokes and repeated softly:

"*For the poor.*"

The eighth stroke had not sounded when this noble and intelligent head fell.

What a wonderful effect public executions have! That same day, while the structure was still standing in their midst, still not washed down, the market traders came out in protest over something to do with tariffs and almost slaughtered a customs official. What gentle people these laws turn you into!

We thought we should tell Claude's Gueux's story in detail, because in our view every paragraph of it could make a chapter heading for a book in which the great problem of the people of the nineteenth century would be solved.

There are two phases in this significant life story: before the fall and after the fall; and within these two phases are two questions: the question of education, the question of punishment; and between these two questions lies the whole of society.

This man was undoubtedly of good birth, well organized, bright. So what did he lack? Give it some thought.

Herein lies the great problem of proportion, whose solution, which has yet to be found, will bring about universal stability: *May society do as much for the individual as nature does.*

Take Claude Gueux. Without doubt he had a good brain, a good heart. But fate put him in such a poorly made society that he ended up stealing; society put him in such a poorly made prison that he ended up killing.

Who is really to blame? Is it him? Or is it us?

Harsh questions, questions that touch us deeply, which appeal to every intelligent mind today, which tug at our coat tails whoever we are, and which will eventually block our path so completely that we ought to look them in the eye and find out what they want.

The writer of these lines might soon attempt to explain how he understands them.

When confronted with facts like these, when you reflect on how these questions plead with us, you wonder what people in government think about if they don't think about this.

The Chamber is incredibly busy all year. It is undoubtedly important to weed out the cushy jobs and prune the budget; it is important to make laws which mean I have to dress up as a soldier and stand guard patriotically outside Monsieur le Comte de Lobau's* gate, someone I don't know and don't want to know, or to make me parade at the Carré Marigny at the whim of my grocer, whom they have made my captain.*

It is important, Deputies and Ministers, to exhaust, to wear out every thing and every idea in this country in fruitless debate; for example, it is vital to put the art of the nineteenth century – that great and austere defendant who chooses not to reply and does well not to do so – in the hot seat, and loudly to question and cross-examine it without knowing what you are talking about; it is of benefit, governors and lawmakers, to spend your time at lectures on the classics which would leave suburban schoolmasters indifferent; it is worthwhile to announce that it is the tragedy of modern times that created incest, adultery, parricide, infanticide and poisoning, thereby proving you don't know your Phaedrus, your Jocasta, or Oedipus, Medea, or Rodogune; it is essential for this country's political speakers to spend three days quarrelling with someone or other over Corneille and Racine, and to make the most of this literary event by competing to see who can ram the biggest grammatical mistakes down the other's throat.*

All this is important; although we think there might be things that are more important.

What would the Chamber say if, in the middle of one of those petty squabbles that so often pit a minister against the opposition and the opposition against a minister, someone suddenly got up from the benches of the Chamber or the public gallery – does it matter which? – and pronounced these serious words:*

"Be quiet, whoever you are! Be quiet, all of you who are talking!* You think you're getting to the point, but you aren't!"

The point is this. Recently, not even a year ago, in Pamiers, the Law cut a man to shreds with a pocket knife; in Dijon it just ripped a woman's head off; in Paris it carries out unpublicized executions at the Saint-Jacques Gate. That is the point. Busy yourselves with that. You can quarrel later about whether the National Guard's buttons should be silver or brass, and whether *assurance* is a finer thing than *certainty*.*

Gentlemen of the centre, gentlemen of the extremes, the vast majority of the people are suffering. Whether you call this a republic or a monarchy, the people are suffering. That is a fact.

The people are hungry, the people are cold. Poverty drives them to crime or to vice, depending on their sex. Have pity on the people, whose sons are taken from them by the chain gang and their daughters by the bawdy house. You have too many convicts, too many prostitutes. What do these two cankers prove? That society is riddled with vice. Here you are, doctors at the patient's bedside; deal with his illness.

You don't give this illness the proper treatment. Examine it more closely. The laws you make, when you make them, are just stopgaps, temporary expedients. One half of your statutes are formulaic, the other half experiments. The branding mark was a cauterization that made the wound gangrenous, a senseless punishment, one that sealed and stamped the crime into the criminal for life! Which made the two of them inseparable friends, comrades! Hard labour is a ridiculous abscess that reabsorbs most of the bad blood it draws out, having first made it worse. The death penalty is a barbaric amputation.

Branding mark, hard labour, death penalty: three things that go together. You abolished the branding mark, it makes sense to abolish the rest.* The branding iron, the ball and chain and the guillotine blade are three parts of a syllogism. You took away the branding iron: the ball and chain and the blade no longer make sense. Farinacci may have been monstrous, but he was not absurd.

Demolish this rickety old scale of crimes and punishments for me and rebuild it. Rebuild your sentences, rebuild your laws, rebuild your prisons, rebuild your judges. Bring the law into line with the moral standards of today.

Gentlemen, too many heads are cut off every year in France. Since you are busy making economies, make one there. Since you are keen to axe jobs, axe the executioner. With what you save on eighty executioners you will be able to pay six hundred schoolmasters.

Think about the vast majority of the people. Schools for children, workshops for men. Did you know that of the countries of Europe, France has one of the lowest numbers of inhabitants who can read! What! The Swiss can read, the Belgians can read, the Danes can read, the Greeks can read, the Irish can read, but the French can't read? It's a disgrace.

Go visit the penal colonies. Send for all the chain gangs. Examine them one by one, these men that mankind's laws have cursed. Work out the angle of their profiles, feel their skulls. Beneath the surface of every one of those fallen men lies the beast within him; it is as if each of them is the point of intersection where some animal species meets humanity. Here is a lynx, there is a cat, a monkey, a vulture, here is a hyena. Now in all these malformed heads, the first fault lies with nature, the second with education. What nature sketched out badly, education's efforts at improvement made worse. Turn your attention to that: a good education for the people. As best you can, help these poor minds develop so that the intelligence inside them can grow. A nation's heads are well or badly made, depending on their institutions. Rome and Greece had lofty brows. As much as you can, open the angle of the people's face.

When France is able to read, don't leave the minds you helped grow without guidance. That would be another catastrophe. A little knowledge is a dangerous thing. No. Don't forget there is a wiser book than the *Compère Mathieu,* better-liked than the *Constitutionnel,** more eternal than the charter of 1830; this is the Scriptures. And now a word of explanation.

Whatever you do, the lot of the common people, the masses, of the *majority* will always be comparatively poor, miserable, unhappy. To them goes the hard work, the burdens to push, to haul, to carry. Take a look at the balance: all the pleasures are on the rich man's plate, all the misfortunes on the poor man's. Are these shares not unequal? Should the scales not be tipped and the State along with them? To the lot of the poor, onto that plate full of misfortune, add the certainty of a future in heaven, the desire for eternal happiness, paradise – that magnificent counterweight! You will set the balance straight. The poor man's share will be as big as the rich man's. Jesus knew this, and he knew a lot more about it than Voltaire did.

Give the people who labour and suffer, the people for whom this is a bad world, the belief in a better world that is made for them. Then they will be peaceful, patient. Patience comes from hope.

Sow the Gospel in the villages. One Bible for each and every shack. Let every book and every field yield a virtuous worker.

The man of the people's head, that is the point. This head is full of good seed; use it so you help it develop, make the most of all that virtue possesses which is most enlightened and restrained. With guidance, the man who committed murder on the highway would have been the best servant in the town. This head, the man of the people's head, cultivate it, till it, water it, fertilize it, shed light on it, give it virtue, make use of it; then you will have no need to cut it off.

Note on the Text

These translations of *The Last Day of a Condemned Man* and *Claude Gueux* have been made from the French edition *Le Dernier Jour d'un condamné, suivi de Claude Gueux et de L'Affaire Tapner* (Paris: Livre de Poche, 1999), with a preface by Robert Badinter and a commentary and notes by Guy Rosa.

Notes

p. III, *abhorrescere a sanguine*: "A horror of blood" (Latin).

p. IV, *æs triplex*: "Triple layer of armour" (Latin) – and also, perhaps, although not strictly speaking, triple remuneration.

p. IV, *the Place de Grève*: Square in Paris where public executions took place. Now the Place de l'Hôtel-de-Ville.

p. V, *ponens caput expiravit*: John 19:30: "Then he bowed his head and gave up his spirit."

p. V, *Ulbach's execution*: Louis Ulbach, twenty years old, was executed on 10th September 1827 for murdering a girl in despair at being separated from her.

p. V, *Beccaria*: Cesare Bonesana, Marquese di Beccaria-Bonesana (1738–94), was an Italian philosopher and politician. His well-known treatise on the penal system, *On Crimes and Punishments*, (1764) greatly influenced Jeremy Bentham.

p. VI, *under the column*: Which column is not clear. The Colonne de Juillet, which commemorates the July Revolution, was not conceived until 1833, although a monument near the site of the old Bastille had been discussed since 1792.

p. VI, *a myriology*: Greek Orthodox chant sung by women at the funeral of relatives.

p. VII, *the entire Chamber… eyes*: We do not claim, however, that everything that was said was contemptible. There were one or two praiseworthy remarks. The same as everyone we applauded Monsieur de Lafayette's modest yet serious speech, as well as Monsieur Villemain's outstanding spontaneity. (HUGO'S NOTE)

p. VII, *Four gentlemen*: Polignac, Peyronnet, Chantelauze and Guernon-Ranville, ministers under Charles X, were accused of a coup in 1830 that brought about the July Revolution. To the anger of the public, the right-wing party saved them by proposing to abolish the death penalty and sentencing them to life imprisonment.

p. VII, *Ucalegon is burning*: See *Aeneid* II, l. 311: Ucalegon's house was destroyed when the Achaeans sacked Troy.

p. IX, *Toulon... Clamart*: Toulon was the site of a penal colony. The cemetery at Clamart was where the bodies of executed prisoners were buried.

p. IX, *quoniam... conversionem*: "Because the Holy Synod hopes to convert heretics" (Latin).

p. X, *Ham*: Ham, in Picardie, was the site of a fortress and jail. Louis Napoleon Bonaparte was a prisoner there from 1840 until 1846.

p. X, *On Crimes and Punishments*: See third note for p. v.

p. X, *a mouse from La Fontaine*: See his *Fables* III, l. 18: 'The Cat and the Old Rat'.

p. XI, *at Pamiers*: A reference to the execution of Pierre Hébrard on 12th September 1831, which actually happened at Albi. It was reported in the *Gazette des Tribunaux*, which is where Hugo found the details.

p. XII, *thirty-four*: La Porte says twenty-two, Aubery thirty-four. Monsieur de Chalais kept screaming until the twentieth blow. (HUGO'S NOTE) In 1626 at Nantes, the conspirator Henri de Talleyrand, Comte de Chalais was messily half beheaded, then hacked to death with a cooper's tool. He had been unable to reconcile his triple role as Richelieu's spy, Louis XIII's "favourite" and the lover of Richelieu's great enemy, the Duchesse de Chevreuse.

p. XIII, *honourable works*: The French here is *"exécuteur des hautes œuvres"*: historically a name for the executioner.

p. XIII, *Bicêtre*: Built by Richelieu in 1632 to house disabled soldiers, it soon became a hospice, a reformatory and then a jail and old people's home.

p. XIV, *The Filangieris... Scudérys*: Gaetano Filangieri (1752–88) was a jurist whose work *La scienza della legislazione* is considered by some to be superior to Beccaria's. His ideas were attacked by Giuseppe Grippa, a professor from Salerno. The fame of Pietro Torregiano (1472–1522) as a sculptor increased after he punched Michelangelo. By criticizing Corneille's work, Georges de Scudéry (1601–67) won Richelieu's favour for himself and his own plays.

p. XV, *Farinacci*: Prospero Farinacci (1554–1618) was a notorious Roman judge. As merciless in tracking down offenders as he was in punishing them, he was far from blameless himself. When he was accused of immorality with a young page, Cardinal Salviati had to intervene to secure a pardon for him from Pope Clement VIII.

p. XV, *Montfaucon*: North-east of Paris, it was the principal gallows of the kings of France.

p. XVI, *discite justitiam moniti*: "Learn from my example what justice is" (Latin). See *Aeneid* VI, l. 620. This is what Phlegyas says in Hell when he is punished with a torment of Tantalus.

p. XVI, *Laffemas*: A pitiless magistrate under Richelieu. He appears in Hugo's 1831 play *Marion Delorme*.

p. XVII, *Bellart... Marchangy*: Nicolas François Bellart, who summed up against the Maréchal Ney and Louis Pierre Louvel, who assassinated the Duc de Berry, was a famous public prosecutor. Marchangy, a writer and prosecuting counsel, summed up against the "four sergeants of La Rochelle", among others. A childhood friend of Hugo's was condemned to death *in absentia* at this same trial, part of which Hugo attended.

p. XVII, *Monsieur Sanson*: Charles-Henri Sanson and his son Henri were the latest members from a well-known family of executioners. Charles-Henri guillotined Louis XVI; his son Marie-Antoinette.

p. XIX, *Monsieur Pigault-Lebrun*: Charles Antoine Guillaume Pigault-Lebrun (1753–1853) was a famous and prolific writer of plays and light novels.

p. XX, *Vouglans... Machault*: Two judges noted for their severity.

p. XX, *the savages*: A reference to Tahiti, whose "parliament" had just abolished the death penalty.

p. XXIII, *A Comedy about a Tragedy*: We felt we should include here this preface in dialogue form that appeared in the third edition of *The Last Day of a Condemned Man*. When reading it, one should bear in mind the political, moral and literary objections that surrounded this book's first publication. (PUBLISHER'S NOTE FROM THE 1832 EDITION)

p. XXVIII, *Odds bodkins*: The French exclamation here is *"Corbleu!"*, an untranslatable play on the poet's remark that the monsters have *corps bleus*, or blue bodies.

p. XXVIII, *Tomorrow... seven*: The opening line from *Cromwell,* which caused a scandal. The other references above are to *Hans of Iceland* (1832) and *Odes and Ballads* (1826).

p. XXIX, *Quidquid... erat*: "Everything he tried to say came out in alexandrines" (Latin). This is more or less what Ovid, whose ability was proverbial, said of himself (*Tristia* IV, l. 10).

p. XXXIII, *Damiens*: On 5th January 1757, Robert François Damiens attempted to assassinate Louis XV with a small knife. He was executed three weeks later, with the most atrocious tortures.

p. XXXIII, *And… behaviour*: This quote is in fact from Nicolas Gilbert's (1750–80) first major work, *The Eighteenth Century* (1775), a biting satire in verse on his times. It is also a misquotation: "And the fall of art follows the loss of virtue."

p. 8, *all men… indefinitely*: The quote is from Hugo's own book, *Hans of Iceland*.

p. 10: These two chapters (6 and 7) replace a preface that was missing from the original edition. They state the book's position without concealing the fact that it is fiction – that art has to step in to speak for the condemned man who, like all such wretches, is denied a voice.

p. 15, *1824*: By 1824 the Emperor, who died in 1821, was far more dead than the condemned man who wishes him long life.

p. 15, *Papavoine*: Executed on 25th March 1825 for stabbing two little boys in front of their mother in the Bois de Vincennes.

p. 16, *parricide*: Parricides had their right hand cut off before they were decapitated.

p. 28, *all this*: "All this" refers to everything before the beginning of Chapter 11 at least: "As it is not yet daylight, what shall I do with the night?" But more likely it also refers to the whole text from the start, as suggested in Chapter 8. In this case the condemned man wrote the book in one night, which wholly justifies the title.

p. 33, *the garde nationale*: A citizens' militia disbanded in April 1827. Its re-establishment was discussed by the Chamber on 14th July 1828. But the "news" Hugo has in mind here is that of 5th November 1827, the day after the King's official birthday, when Charles X published a decree dissolving the Chamber and naming a "batch" of peers (seventy-six, the number quoted by the superstitious policeman in Chapter 32). But there is confusion about dates in the book, due to slips on the author's part and the interval between writing and publication. The point Hugo is making is the difference between events that preoccupy the average reader and serious social issues like the death penalty and the mob's backwards attitude to it, which everyday events conceal.

p. 35, *printed sheets*: These are execution announcements being sold. In Chapter 43 the condemned man's small daughter reads one out to show him she can read.

p. 36, *friauche*: The origins of this expression are almost as obscure in French as they are to an English speaker. Despite much research into the etymology of slang, it has never been wholly established whether Hugo invented the word or heard it on one of his visits to Bicêtre.

p. 37, *Charlot*: The executioner.

p. 37, *shifties*: Hands. (Slang use of *louches* in the original.)

p. 37, *digger*: Pocket. (Slang use of *fouilleuse*.)

p. 37, *peel*: Overcoat. (Slang use of *pelure*.)

p. 37, *wide boy*: Crook. (Slang use of *marlou*.)

p. 37, *babbling brook*: Thief.

p. 37, *I bust open a boutie, I bent a turn*: I broke into a shop, I copied a key. (Slang use of *boutanche* and *tournante*.)

p. 37, *crow's floorcloth*: A priest's cassock.

p. 37, *crouch*: Live. (*Tapiquer*, a slang expression.)

p. 37, *an old lag*: One who has been sent back to the penal colony.

p. 37, *the green caps*: Convicts sentenced to hard labour for life.

p. 38, *pitch and toss*: Leader, boss. (*Coire*, a slang expression.)

p. 38, *relieving on the frog*: Murdering and robbing on the highways.

p. 38, *snare merchants*: The police.

p. 38, *the reaper*: The executioner.

p. 38, *married the widow*: Was hung.

p. 38, *Abbey of Mount-Sorrow*: The guillotine.

p. 38, *Don't come the chicken in front of the bulldog*: Don't be a coward when faced with death.

p. 39, *the boar*: The priest.

p. 50, *a thou*: In the original "*un millier*", a common nineteenth-century French expression for 1,000 pounds, or 500 kilos.

p. 53, *the seven letters of his name*: Charles (X).

p. 67, *Claude Gueux*: Based on real events and first published in 1834, it tells the tragic story of the title character, a poor Parisian worker who is forced to steal in order to survive.

p. 70, *He... other*: The image that Hugo evokes here is based on theories about the human capacity for warmth current at the end of the eighteenth and early nineteenth centuries, the belief that there was fluid in the body that transmitted warmth, both physical and emotional. Similarly, the earlier reference to a "variety of the species" comes from the natural sciences.

p. 72, *Signor de Cotadilla*: A personal memory of the author's. De Cotadilla was in charge of the escort for the convoy of vehicles on Hugo's journey across Spain in 1811.

p. 80, *Jacques Clément*: Jacques Clément (1567–89) was a fanatical Dominican monk who assassinated Henri III in 1589. On the pretext of having a secret message for him he was granted a private audience with the King, whom he then stabbed to death. He was killed on the spot by royal guards. His corpse was publicly quartered and burnt.

p. 84, *Article 296*: Article 296 of the Criminal Code states: "Any killing committed with premeditation or by means of a trap is treated as murder." And Article 302: "Anyone guilty of murder, parricide, infanticide or poisoning will be punished by death."

p. 85, *the defendant was called Gueux*: In French, *gueux* can mean "beggar", "rogue", "villain", etc., as well as being a surname.

p. 86, *pede claudo*: A reference to *Pede pœna claudo*, meaning "punishment comes limping". In the *Odes* III, l. 2, this is how Horace describes a just punishment: always late but inevitable.

p. 86, *According... away*: This is the account that appeared in the *Gazette des Tribunaux* of 15th June 1832, which mentioned a "bloodthirsty remark" but no overt use of force.

p. 88, *le Comte de Lobau's*: Lobau was Commander of the National Guard in Paris, the reforming of which was one of the victories of the bourgeois revolt of 1830. It proved its military worth repeatedly against rebellious workers, especially in June 1848.

p. 88, *dress up as a soldier... captain*: Needless to say we have no intention of criticizing the urban patrol, a useful thing that safeguards the streets, the hearth and home, but only parades, dressing up, military vanity and oompah-oompah, which just turn a citizen into a caricature of a soldier. (HUGO'S NOTE)

p. 88, *It is important... throat*: In May 1834, a debate in the Chamber about the budget – including subsidies for theatres – provided the opportunity for long harangues that aimed to curb the "licentiousness" of theatres (in particular the plays of Adolphe Dumas) with a reintroduction of censorship.

p. 88, *What... words*: This is the beginning of a passage that is linked to the narrative by the three preceding paragraphs, and which was written prior to the story of Claude Gueux.

p. 88, *Be quiet... talking!*: The first edition, which named the spokesmen for the right and the left, put it more bluntly: "Shut up, Monsieur Mauguin! Shut up, Monsieur Thiers!"

p. 89, *You... certainty*: On 15th April 1831, the government had the word "certainty" altered to "hope" in a motion voted in the Chamber to the effect that "the Polish Nation would not perish".

p. 89, *You... rest*: The law of 28th April 1832 modified several articles in the French penal code: it abolished the use of the branding mark, the iron collar and the cutting off of a parricide's right hand.

p. 90, *Compère Mathieu... Constitutionnel*: *Le Compère Mathieu* was one of the many, sometimes weighty annuals read by the proletariat. The dull and respectable newspaper *Le Constitutionnel* was read by the bourgeoisie.

  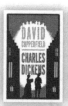

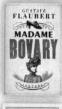